CW00468476

## About the Author

Peter has always opened up his imagination to creative challenges. Having spent most of his professional career surrounded by a wide variety of top-line creative individuals ranging from visualisers, illustrators and copywriters within product brand development, he concedes that by being in close proximity to such talents for so long that some of it has 'rubbed-off' on him finally being able to put pen to paper as a 'surreal' story writer. This is his first published children's novel. He lives in Warrington, Cheshire, with his wife Pauline.

# Professor Peregrine Greylag and the Three Keys of Didsvale Park

Peter J Hossack-Gilberts

# Professor Peregrine Greylag and the Three Keys of Didsvale Park

Olympia Publishers
*London*

**www.olympiapublishers.com**
OLYMPIA PAPERBACK EDITION

First Published in 2023

**Olympia Publishers
Tallis House
2 Tallis Street
London
EC4Y 0AB**

Printed in Great Britain

# Dedication

To Olive Mary and Nellie Mae

# Acknowledgements

Thank you to my own 'Pretty Pol', without your loving support this particular ship would never have sailed and been navigated away from the treacherous hidden rocks that may have been awaiting me in the deepest of seas. To my loving and amazing family, close friends and inspirations from the past. Oh! And a special 'thank you' to Professor Peregrine Greylag for knowing I was going to write this story about him before I did!

# Introduction

The fresh new sticker clearly showed a company name within a distinct, professionally designed, colourful logo displaying '*Underpinning Inc.*'. Carefully peeling it back from the cab door on the huge white commercial lorry, and just about distinguishable, was revealed a handwritten word, '*DRONES*'. Professor Peregrine Greylag's inquisitive nature was suddenly disturbed by an electronic buzzing noise from inside as the top of the lorry slowly began to open upwards. He reacted as fast as he could and pressed the sticker back into its original position, jumped onto his bicycle and desperately sped along the forest path towards the safety of the engine shed. The whirring black objects, which had ascended from within the lorry, swooped behind him and quickly closed in as he pedalled faster and faster through the trees of the nature reserve. Frantically rushing across a river bridge, he kicked out vengefully at a warning sign with such force that it spun around several times. With their single oval scarlet receptor panels giving the menacing appearance of flying red devil-eyed monsters, the squadron of black drones and their larger queen drone relentlessly caught up with their prey, forcing him to weave in and out of the trees until he finally lost control of his bicycle and somersaulted into the giant tree trunk of the mighty oak tree of Didsvale Park. The sinister looking drones then whirred off into the distance and back to their base—

mission accomplished! A gigantic figure rushed from the nearby trees to see what all the commotion was about. It bent over the forlorn figure of the professor, listening to his final utterances. The professor gave one last familiar smile at the helpful figure as his last breath was taken. As he did so, a lone jackdaw cawed mournfully in the dense leafy canopy high above him and shed a single black feather, which swirled slowly downwards before gently resting onto the face of the now lifeless figure lying beneath.

# Chapter 1
## Several Months Later

Several giant saltwater droplets cascaded down and landed onto the Adamson's framed photograph, tightly grasped by the onlooker whose tears began to flood the glass surface. Then, slowly wiping away the drops from his face with the back of his hand before they could join the other tears he had shed, his sad mood oddly changed as he began to take on a broad smile at his find.

The solitary figure bent down, delving deeper and deeper into the cardboard box that he had found damaged and burst open lying against a nearby tree, hidden well out of view from the doorstep where they were obviously intended to belong, he thought. A number of personal framed mementos had appeared and been carefully scrutinised before he reached a family photograph at the bottom of the box. It was met with the long, intriguing, mumbled, rhetorical question, "Mmmmmm. What do we have here then, I wonder?"

Voices could then be heard approaching in the distance. The box's ripped brown tape fastening was then quickly rewound, making it secure once again, and the box was then left on the cottage doorstep where it could easily be noticed. The mysterious figure then scurried off in a hurry without being noticed.

During their late summer holiday break, Toby, Libby and

Olive were in the process of moving to the area and into their quaint rented accommodation, Kingfisher Cottage, an old gatehouse lodge situated outside the main open entrance to Didsvale Manor. They had earlier approached the front door, armed with boxes and other possessions, to be greeted by a hanging hand-painted sign—**Welcome to Kingfisher Cottage—'Enter and Dream'**. It had a colourfully detailed drawing of a kingfisher on it. "Not bad…" commented Libby, judging the sign's artistic contents, "…couldn't have done better myself," she added.

All three then made their way into the cottage and started to unpack before taking a welcome break from the many exhaustive cardboard storage boxes. As they returned, Toby said, "Well, that was a nice refreshing breather of a walk. Let's get back to moving into our new abode." He then spotted that an extra box had mysteriously been placed on their doorstep. "That's odd. This wasn't here when we left," as he carefully lifted up the newly found box. "The removal men must have forgotten to unload it and brought it back while we were out. Just as well. Look!" He pointed to the felt tip marking on the side, which read '**Adamsons—Private & Confidential**'. "One of our most valuable storage boxes nearly went missing," he added, with great relief.

"All's well that ends well," Libby said philosophically as they entered the house.

# Chapter 2
## Olive's Premonition!

Outside the lodge, the bright, sunny, fresh daytime was quickly giving way to the dusk of the rapidly arriving evening. Silhouetted against the open sky background were hundreds of thousands of birds twisting and turning high above Kingfisher Cottage, like black smoke swirling in a hurricane. The Adamsons' eight-year-old daughter, Olive, had been resting asleep with her head supported on her arms on the windowsill in her new bedroom. She looked out of the window to see a magnificent display of thousands and thousands of starlings writing out the words *OLIVE*... and then... *WELCOME TO KINGFISHER COTTAGE*... with their swooping shapes in the sky. Immediately afterwards, she saw a strange single large black crow with a multi-coloured head swoop beneath her window towards the front door, where it rested for a few seconds before flying away at ground level into the nearby trees.

Olive ran with excitement down the stairs to her parents still busy unpacking— "Mum! Dad! Guess what I saw?"

"No, what?" said her mum.

"The starlings wrote to me in the sky and a giant black crow with a multi-coloured head came to our front door," she exclaimed with excitement.

"Has she been dreaming while resting?" asked Toby of

Libby as they looked at the clear blue sky outside with no detection of what Olive had described. "What do you mean—wrote to you? And what's this about a giant crow?"

"No, I wasn't dreaming. Honestly!" Olive insisted.

"Remember what it says on the door, Olive. 'Enter and Dream'. I think you've done exactly that in your short nap!" Libby reasoned.

Toby suddenly jumped back into the conversation. "Errm, maybe I can offer an explanation." He reached into his back pocket and brought out a piece of folded paper. "I forgot to mention. I found this on the hallway doormat earlier. Someone must have posted it and kindly not bothered to knock so they wouldn't disturb us packing. Anyway, I reckon it was delivered by Olive's odd looking crow before scooting off unannounced."

Olive turned to her mother. "See!" She claimed victoriously.

# Chapter 3
## The Invitation

"OK Let's just see what we have here then," said Toby in anticipation as he unfolded the piece of paper found earlier on the doormat. They were all now relaxing comfortably in the lounge as he began to read out the note in his hand.

*"'PRIVATE INVITATION'*
*Libby, Toby & Olive Adamson are invited to a performance*
*from the Younoseeme Squibrels and a grand tour of*
*Didsvale Park and Nature Reserve*
*— TONIGHT! 7.30 p.m. —*
*— Captain Ahab McCrab— 'Park Keeper!' —*
*(Knock on the side door seven times, then pause seven*
*seconds for knock number eight. Please don't forget and*
*don't be late!)"*

"Can we go to visit the park and watch the Younoseeme Squibrels?" Olive pleaded as she turned to each parent for agreement. "Pleeeeeeease?" she begged.

"Yes, let's," added her mum. "Whatever they are. Sounds fun! And by way of a personal invitation no less! It's nice that someone has taken the time and consideration to welcome us into the area. Hopefully, we'll all be refreshed by seven-thirty... and free from sleepy hallucinations!" she added, with a warm smile directed at Olive. "Remember the instruction, Olive," she reminded. "We must 'knock on the side door seven times, then pause seven seconds for knock number eight. Please don't forget and don't be late'," she added in a hoity-toity voice.

"Absolutely," confirmed Toby, "...it sounds quite interesting and entertaining. Maybe we'll meet Olive's mythical giant crow with the colourful head?" he added humorously, before running around the room flapping imaginary wings and screeching 'caw, caw, caw' sounds at the top of his voice to the joint laughter of the others.

# Chapter 4
## Meeting the Captain

Later on, they all arrived at Didsvale Park and approached a large set of tall wooden gates. A notice was pinned to one of them, written by hand in black paint. It read…

**ALL PERFORMANCES CANCELLED—PARK CLOSED UNTIL FURTHER NOTICE—SORRY FOR ANY INCONVENIENCE—HEAD KEEPER**

"Strange," said Libby quizzically to Toby. "Closed? Why have we been invited to a closed park? Must be some kind of practical joke. Oh well, let's go home."

"Let's not give up that easily, Mum. At least let me try the knocking code," begged Olive.

"OK, go ahead, but I think we may be wasting our time," Libby agreed.

Olive didn't need a second chance, as she leapt at the door and knocked seven times as the invitation had stated until reaching the last part… *"then pause seven seconds for knock number eight,"* which she carried out patiently and then waited… and waited… Then, just as they turned round to walk away, a loud thud came as the park gates began to creek open. Libby and Toby looked at each other sheepishly before jointly shrugging their shoulders and entering cautiously through the open gates. No sooner were they inside the park than the gates suddenly and mysteriously swung back and locked behind them. In the gathering dusk ahead of them twinkling lights could be made out along the pathway. Every so often they came across a weather-worn litterbin with a handwritten note stuck to it with an arrow pointing further along the path —

## —TOBY, LIBBY & OLIVE—THIS WAY PLEASE!—

They hadn't gone more than a few paces before Toby strayed off the pathway and suddenly tripped forward over a hidden obstacle. "What on earth...?" he exclaimed to the others. "Looks like some old planks of wood and a bit of rusting railway track in this undergrowth. Looks like it's been under here for quite some time!" He bent down to pick up a smaller length of wood from the long grass and read out the brightly coloured lettering and queried, "'**Didsvale Park Station**'? That's peculiar. It appears there was a train station here at some time."

"Never mind, Toby. We can ask about that later. Let's keep going," Libby said encouragingly. Following more similar litterbin directions they progressed to an area that opened up into a large glade dominated by a gigantic oak tree, eerily silhouetted against the closing twilight evening, where they came to a stop.

"Wow, what a tree," remarked Libby. "How enchanting. Never seen one as big as that before with so many twisting branches. They look like spooky arms stretching out, don't they? It looks ancient. This glade looks like some kind of amphitheatre to me, with this mighty specimen of a tree as the backdrop," she guessed further. Suddenly, she diverted her attention to a bunch of flowers at the base of the tree. "Aww, look. How sad. It looks like someone's left a memorial bouquet at the base. It looks private so we shouldn't pry," she said sympathetically to Olive.

No sooner had Libby got the words out of her mouth, the branches and leaves in front of them started to shake and sway suddenly as though something was moving through them. Then, from above, the air was filled with a strange calypso singing rhythm, with no evidence of where it was coming from. Olive stopped suddenly on the path. "Shhhh!" she ordered her parents by putting her finger to her lips. "Listen!" she demanded with a loud whisper so they could all hear singing coming from the branches and leaves of the giant oak tree.

*"We're the Younoseeme Squibrels of Didsvale Park,*
*swaying in the branches from dawn till dark. Chatting and*
*a singing while you walk around, though you'll never ever*
*see us in the sky or on the ground.*
*You may hear us in the trees or maybe by the stream—or*
*was it when asleep in a lazy, hazy dream.*
*Through Winter, Spring, Summer to the Autumn Fall, the*
*Younoseeme Squibrels will entertain you all."*

Then they heard more singing…

*"You put your left arm in, your left arm out*
*In, out, in, out, you shake it all about*
*You do the hokey cokey and you turn around*
*That's what it's all about*
*Woah, the hokey cokey*

*Woah, the hokey cokey*
*Woah, the hokey cokey*
*Knees bent*
*Arms stretched*
*Ra-ra-ra*
*You put your right arm in…"*

The singing began to stop as fast as it began, before the branches and leaves above rustled and swayed again as if something was rushing through them and hurried away before everything became still again! "What on earth was that? How weird. There wasn't a single breeze when we came in," Toby mused.

"Never mind that, Dad. I know exactly what it was. It was the magic singing of the Younoseeme Squibrels, here to entertain us!" claimed Olive.

"It'll probably be some kind of loudspeaker mechanism with pulleys and wires set off by a trip wire, I'd imagine. I bet this was the cancelled 'performance' mentioned on the gate notice. Whoever had organised it has just forgotten to switch it off. There's always an explanation to these tricks!" reasoned Toby. "Onwards!" He beckoned to the others.

"Well, we know it was magic. Don't we, Olive?" Libby said to Olive to appease her, without confessing that she really agreed with Toby's words of common sense.

"Yes," Olive replied, "and I'm going to have these magic souvenirs. Look!" She picked up a piece of broken oak tree branch and several small acorns from under the tree. Waving the branch, she declared, "Look. It's in a 'Y' shape. 'Y' for Younoseeme!" she stated cleverly, as she placed the souvenir items into her top dungaree pocket for safekeeping.

As they approached a clump of trees, the ghostly sound of a chain being dragged along the ground came slowly from behind them. Toby and Libby stopped, rigid with fright, awaiting the approaching spectre's appearance. Libby held a protective hand over Olive's eyes in anticipation.

Suddenly, a giant figure loomed from behind a wooden cabin, dragging a length of rusty old chain behind it. "Oh, sorry. I didn't mean to startle you?" apologised the ghostly figure to the three park guests. "Doing a little bit more landscaping to my nautical garden on my way to meet you all," said the figure to the Adamsons. Please... follow me..." he beckoned.

"This must be Captain Ahab. Isn't he funny?" Olive whispered excitedly to the other two as they straggled behind, trying to keep up with the enormous figure pacing out in front of them.

"Guess so," replied her dad with a hint of uneasiness.

The party proceeded along a dirt path, which passed a dilapidated old café alongside a narrow river. The pathway was lit by nautical lanterns dangling on both sides, and had just started twinkling in the early evening dusk. Adjacent to the path was more evidence of an old railway track lying in the undergrowth, part of which diverted across a wooden bridge across the river to the other side. A rusting piece of metal could be made out, which poked out from the undergrowth. "Look!" burst out Toby. "The railway track diverts over that bridge. There's the rusty old lever for it," as he pointed out enthusiastically to the points control lever. "Doesn't look very inviting over there, though," as he nodded towards a sign pitched on the other side of the bridge displaying the wording 'DANGER—KEEP OUT—SINKHOLES'.

They continued onwards with the track just about evident to their side. The giant figure strode on, with the party struggling behind. Toby turned to Libby. "Blimey. He doesn't hang around, does he? Look, there's even more of that old railway track."

"Yes. I noticed," she replied.

Another few hundred yards along the pathway into the woodland appeared a large wooden hut with the words '*Bosun's Cabin*' roughly engraved by hand on a wooden sign that hung down by the doorway. On the other side of the doorway hung a large, gleaming, solid brass bell, which had obviously been lovingly polished by the way it sharply reflected the distorted image of the onlookers' faces as they approached. Engraved along the bottom edge of the bell were the words 'Pretty Pol'. This is where they all came to a stop and where Captain Ahab gently lowered the old rope effortlessly to the floor and began to speak again. "This rope is another useful donation left for me at the old ferry landing!" Then, pointing to the bell, said mysteriously, "Next time you'll all need to remember this very important rhyme… '*As the last of eight bells ends its ring, mighty Argyll will take to wing. He'll billow your sails and give you speed, to Pamona Atoll for the juice you need*'," whilst giving his nose repeated taps indicating that he was confiding in the Adamsons to share his secret.

"What's that supposed to mean? Which island? What juice? I hope you remembered all of that," whispered Libby to Toby out of earshot from the captain.

"*I* did!" whispered Olive confidently to her parents. She then repeated the words to them. "'*As the last of eight bells*

24

*ends its ring, mighty Argyll will take to wing. He'll billow your sails and give you speed, to Pamona Atoll for the juice you need.'* I think you can safely leave that with me," she insisted smartly.

"OK. We'll leave that in your control, Olive," agreed her parents.

On closer inspection, the garden outside the hut was themed with an array of nautical objects and artefacts, adorned by a glorious display of flowers and plants flourishing brightly within it. There was a bird feeding area similarly designed in quirky nautical fashion made from a variety of things such as lobster cages, rope, brass instruments of every description and numerous nautical lanterns suspended from the tree branches above. Ahab then brought an authentic bosun's whistle from his pocket and put it to his lips. It was the type of traditional whistle that was used to invite special guests on board ship, except he was pretending to invite today's special guests, the Adamsons, into his hut! He began to pipe them all aboard ceremoniously, while his other hand swept theatrically across the name on the sign for him to make the following announcement, "It gives me great pleasure to welcome the Adamson family to Bosun's Cabin!" He gestured again with an over-dramatic sweeping gesture of his mighty hand inviting them one by one through the open doorway. As they stood inside the dimly lit cabin he continued. "Forgive my rudeness. I forgot to introduce myself, didn't I? I'm Captain Ahab McCrab—that's McCrab spelt with a small 'c' before a capital 'C'. It's easy as that to remember. Just think of the Atlantic Sea followed by the Irish Sea! Get it! A big sea followed by a small sea! Get it? The letter '**C**' and the word '**SEA**'. Ha! ha! ha! Hee! hee! hee!" he added with uncontrolled laughter. The

Adamsons looked confused but laughed in any case so as not to offend their eccentric host, who then pointed to a silver tankard sitting on the shelf opposite depicting an anchor with his name confirming the spelling. "Please call me Ahab." He then gestured for all three to sit on separate chairs. Toby and Libby took their places, while Olive struggled as she squirmed and fidgeted to get comfortable once she had positioned herself up to the same height as the other two. The captain then struck a match and lit several oil lamps, which illuminated the dim cabin to reveal more of its fascinating nautical character. "It's always a little gloomy in here and this place doesn't have any electricity, I'm glad to say. Old fashioned that's me," he concluded.

Toby, Libby and Olive's attention strayed into each and every corner of the room just as Ahab suddenly brought them back to his attention, where they would soon be utterly transfixed for a good while. "Sorry I couldn't greet you at the gate. I was preoccupied as you could see. I really didn't intend to scare you," he said apologetically. "I'm glad you remembered the secret password!"

"That was down to me!" Olive said proudly. "How does it work when you're not around?"

"OK. So that you know next time, Olive. It's a quirky invention and done by sound waves. There's some kind of sensor box at the base of the old railway signal by the gate. It connects with the signal arm, which releases the gate catch when you knock the secret enter knock! When you knocked eight times on the park gate side door it opened automatically. But you must keep the code secret and never divulge it to another soul," he added, putting a single finger to his lips. Olive copied the silent gesture in agreement back to Ahab.

26

"Did you invent it, Ahab?" Olive quizzed further.

"No, not me, Olive. I'm nowhere near to be that clever. But I'll tell you who was soon enough. Anyway… I'm so glad you all accepted my special personal invitation here to Didsvale Park!"

Out of pure curiosity and for not being easily duped for her age, Olive couldn't resist asking, "I thought the 'Younoseeme Squibrels' performance was A-mazing, Captain Ahab. How is it done? Is it a trick?"

The captain looked at her with an amount of surprised disdain. "How is it done? Trick? Not everything you see or experience in Didsvale Park and Nature Reserve is done as a trick, Olive, he insisted. "I'll let you know more about that loveable pair of entertaining rascals later."

Olive looked sideways and whispered to her parents as Ahab briefly looked away. "Well, I did ask!" she said while shrugging her shoulders and pulling a facial expression of resignation.

The captain began, "I must ask that you trust everything I say to you as complete fact and not fiction. First of all, I do apologise for enticing you all here by virtue of my invitation, but what I am about to reveal is the ulterior motive behind the invitation. The very fact that you have accepted it and arrived here is nothing but confirmation to me that the fates have conspired and I know without a shadow of doubt that there's a genuine reason for you being here. So, if you are all sitting comfortably, then I'll begin."

The captivated audience nodded solidly in agreement as one as they waited.

Ahab settled back in his authentic captain's chair. "Here's my little tale then." He paused a little before starting. "I wangled my way into the merchant navy from school at the age of fifteen and left for distant horizons, spending most of my life from that day 'married to the oceans'. So after many happy years of sailing on the high seas to all corners of the globe, I decided to retire and took up the position of ferryman at Didsvale Ferry about a mile down the River Babble, which happens to flow through the park. With permission from Lord and Lady Greylag, who owned it, the ferry was used to take visitors across to the manor estate and nature reserve, and back again. I say the word 'ferry' in the loosest of terms. It was a crude conversion of Professor Greylag's exploration sailboat, '*Pretty Pol*' that he allowed the park to use as the ferry, and what I used to steer and propel from the back with the aid of a large pole. You could describe it as a crude version of the punts you see going up and down the river at Cambridge, except this vessel carried up to six passengers at a time. It needed some strength to row, I tell you, as you had to fight the fast waters and currents of the river on occasions, although it never gave me any problems. Over the years, I counted every passenger across, and every one of them back again!" he stated proudly and reassuringly before continuing. "There was a small hut by the ferry, which I used to live in. However, once the new Lord Didsvale moved in, that was the end of the ferry and my accommodation. He said that we were now surplus to requirements and that he had new plans for the estate. Professor Greylag took pity on my plight and offered me the position of head keeper here at the park, with free accommodation in return. I couldn't believe my luck!" he stated before quickly moving on. "You may wonder where all these bit and pieces come from," pointing at the various nautical artefacts around the room. "Well, there's a small beach a few miles downstream where the River Babble meets the open sea at the estuary. My old seafaring shipmates would leave them there as they passed by on their ships sailing back from around the world. They would give four blasts of their horn to let me know when something had been left. I would scoot down there with my handcart, load up and bring them back every now and then. Over a period of my time, I assembled quite an array of useful, discarded nautical bits and pieces. The more the sailors knew of my collection, the more and more discarded items were left me from breakers yards around the globe until I had too much and just couldn't take any more. It was a sad day when I had to leave my message in the sandy beach to say *'thank you but no more, my seafaring friends'*! When the ferry closed, I still brought everything up here on the handcart bit by bit and when my new home was finally adorned, Professor Greylag thought it was very fitting that I called this little place 'Bosun's Cabin'. After all, I had everything needed to spend my time restoring each item back to life again and decorate this lovely cabin with them. Alas, my trusty old handcart eventually gave way to the rigours of time and became irreparable, so I decided to use it for firewood to keep the cabin warm." At this point, Ahab ended his narration and became lost in thought, scanning around his works of art. The onlookers' eyes tracked his every move up and down and side to side, and all nodded once again in unison with complimentary smiles.

During the introduction to his tale, Toby, Libby and Olive had more time to inspect the captain's appearance, which was as close to an unconventional seafarer's profile as one could imagine, with a weatherworn face finished off with a large white bushy beard, and long wavy hair with a ponytail to match. Sat steadily on top of his head was a captain's hat adorned with a bright silver badge made in the shape of a ship's anchor. Still legible, but slightly frayed despite many obvious years of wear and tear were gold embroidered words on the front of his hat spelling out the name *S.S. Pretty Pol*.

His enormous frame was clothed in a grey and white stripy t-shirt underneath a blue waistcoat, interrupted on either side by a pair of wide blue braces patterned with continuous lines of tiny white anchors holding up a large baggy pair of orangey-red waterproof trousers. A pair of enormous feet protruded out of the bottom of his pants, clad in a sturdy pair of black boots.

While Ahab was still distracted telling his story, Libby turned to Toby and whispered, "Quite a character our Captain Ahab!"

"Quite," agreed Toby, who continued to look around, taking in the most imaginative nautical décor in the guise of ships' lanterns, old rusty anchors of various sizes, ships' wheels, binnacles, assortments of brass objects, chests, rope netting, ladders, porthole windows, brass pipes, clocks, capstans and lots of teak coloured varnished wood covering the floors, walls and ceiling. Anything and everything that could be found on a ship seemed to be part of the bizarre interior of the cabin. It was an absolute treasure trove. He whispered back to Libby and joked, "I feel like I'm on the high seas and getting a little sea queasy. Is there a spare bucket around?"

Olive overheard the disrespectful remark from her parents and glared at them both with disdain. She had taken an obvious shine to this new character being introduced to her family. They looked back with obvious discomfort and embarrassment as their young daughter continued to glare at them.

Ahab regained his concentration on his guests and continued with a loud interjection. "**So**! This evening I'd like to formerly welcome the Adamson family, Toby, Libby and Olive, to their new residence at Kingfisher Cottage and also here at Didsvale Park. As you can see, I've spent some time and care to make my abode a little bit like my home from home," he concluded.

The three nodded again, this time with even more accentuated agreement.

The captain continued. "See those over there." He pointed to a small recess in the corner of the cabin. They could see two identical shiny closed wooden doors, each featuring a small glass porthole at the top. "Those came from an old French aircraft carrier," he added. "My sleeping quarters are through there, and the teak wood that you see on the floor, walls and ceiling of this cabin...? that all comes from various discarded vessels brought back to me by my old shipmates from the ship breakers yards around the globe. Faraway places such as Chittagong, otherwise known as 'the maritime breakers graveyard of Bangladesh'!"

"Wow!" came a cry of fascination from Olive. "Do you mind if I have look?" she asked the captain.

"Of course not. Be my guest." He gestured for Olive to go over to the interesting shiny double-doors. She quickly went to inspect, then using her tiptoes to peek through one of the portholes. Expecting to see a bedroom at least the same size as her own bedroom, she was surprised to see a much smaller area with a hammock suspended from both sides taking up much of the space. She then took on a very thoughtful expression at what she saw next. In the opposite corner were two tiny hammocks, each one just a couple of feet in length. She could also see a small ship's light set in a metal frame attached to the wall. Affixed to the other wall was a bookshelf with an array of nautical themed books arranged from end to end. In the corner was an old tea chest with the words—'THE EAST INDIA COMPANY' which she assumed Ahab used as his table.

Olive returned and climbed back onto her chair. "Are you not uncomfortable sleeping in there, Captain Ahab?" she asked. "It looks very..." she hesitated, looking for the right description so as not to offend... "very... cosy...!"

"No, not at all," responded the captain. Once I get swaying on those imaginary waves on the high seas again, I'm asleep for oceans and oceans of hours!"

"Hee! Hee! Hee!" Olive chuckled at Ahab's explanation. "Are those two tiny hammocks souvenirs from your travels?" she quizzed.

"No, not at all. That's where the Younoseeme Squirbels sleep. I call them their shammocks! You didn't disturb them, I hope? They'll be having a deserved rest after the performance they gave for you all earlier!" he explained.

"But there was nothing in those sham...?" Olive was cut off abruptly in mid-sentence before she could challenge his explanation.

"...Not only that, Olive," Ahab continued to focus on his sceptical listener. "They're extra tired today as they've been collecting new batches of fallen leaves from the Mighty Oak tree and taking them back and forth to the engine shed all day for the preparation of the next batch of special magicmunchymulch. Strange though!" he mused to himself with a serious expression. "They're still taking it, very loyally, despite the fact that the professor is no longer with us. They must know something we don't. Very intuitive are those Younoseeme Squibrels. Old habits die hard I suppose!" he concluded.

Not to be outdone, Olive tried again to question Ahab's strange explanation. "What do you mean by special magicmunchy...?"

Once again, and before she could hardly get the last word from her lips, Ahab abruptly cut her dead to change the subject completely. "See those captain's chairs you're sat on?" He nodded to each of the gleaming steel stools with leather seats and armrests supporting them. "They came from the bridges of three old navy frigates. Imagine that, Olive!" He singled her out for a response.

"Wow!" she answered in surprise.

"And just outside, when you entered my cabin, you may have noticed my snaking chains, ropes and rockery. Well, the chains and ropes represent the eels that travel from the Sargasso Sea, and the rockery represents the Key West archipelago of America," the captain stated proudly at his creation. "See all those swirly patterns made from old ship's rope," he pointed, "well, they are there to remind me of all the tides and currents of the oceans, and the pretty flowers amongst them are all the weird and wonderful colourful fish I've seen and swum with over the years!"

"It's very impressive, Captain Ahab," Libby responded from her own creative judgement.

Out of the blue, Olive suddenly asked Ahab a pointed question. "How... did... you... know where we lived, Captain Ahab?"

"Well. That's a very good question to ask, Olive, and one I was waiting for," he replied mysteriously, staring directly at Olive with a solitary finger pressed to his lips. "Let's just say that a little bird told me."

Libby took a deep inward gasp as she remembered the words Olive said she saw written in the starling murmuration formation through her bedroom window at the cottage earlier that day. Perhaps 'Welcome to Kingfisher Cottage' wasn't a dream after all she thought to herself.

The captain continued. "And those little birds also told me that you, Toby, work from home as a chemical engineering consultant and enjoy flying light aircraft. You also love railways, as I'm well informed? Very impressive!" he added admiringly.

"Well, yes, but how…?" replied Toby in astonishment before he was suddenly cut off by Ahab's silencing finger-to-lip motion.

"And you, Libby, are a much-travelled wildlife naturalist, botanist and acclaimed illustrator. I'm thrilled to meet you too," Ahab added with further admiration.

"Well, yes, but how on earth…?" replied Libby similarly shocked before she was cut off in exactly the same way by Ahab's silencing finger.

"Now you know how I feel," whispered Toby empathetically to Libby unnoticed by Ahab as he continued his weird mind-reading assessment and focussing onto Olive.

"And you, Olive…!" He looked at the startled youngster, "You love writing stories and want to be a great author in the future. You will go anywhere your imagination takes you, swept along with on a current of brain waves!"

Olive nodded eagerly with amazement.

Before continuing, Ahab sighed and took in a deep breath with a look of indignation… "I'm afraid I have a confession and apology to make to you all," he continued with the Adamsons hooked onto his every word. "I'm not the mind-reader you may think I am after all, but in reality, I actually found your framed mementos earlier this morning in a box by your cottage before I delivered your invitation afterwards. I didn't mean to pry but… the box had split open and was in such a sorry state, that I couldn't help but notice the content as I repaired it and left it back on the doorstep for you to find. It was the content of the box that convinced me to return later on my bike. I quickly posted your invitation without being noticed. I hope you can forgive me?" he urged.

"Well, of course we do. Don't we?" Libby looked for support from the others, which came immediately. "But why didn't you knock on the door and say hello?" she quizzed.

"Because I needed you to come because of your own intrigue and intuition. If I'd asked you directly, you may have said *no*. Besides, this is the one and only place where I would feel comfortable telling my story to you," Ahab emphasised its importance as he explained to the puzzled listeners.

"No—please don't feel bad Captain Ahab," Libby added. "There's no need to apologise. If we hadn't taken up your kind invitation, we wouldn't be sat here in your wonderful…" she hesitated for a quick second while looking around for a fitting complimentary description and carefully mumbled out the words, "… incredible nautical treasure trove."

Captain Ahab smiled proudly and was oblivious to Libby's well chosen, tactful response. "Well, thank you. I've spent some time assembling it to my liking, as you can see."

Just as Ahab was finishing his words, Olive had returned

to Ahab's sleeping quarters for a closer inspection. Hanging there from a coat hook in the shape of fish's heads was a long black cloak on one hook and a multi-coloured school cap positioned on top. She took a sudden gasp and excitedly turned around towards Ahab. "It was you! It was you!" she exclaimed even louder. "You were the giant black crow with the multi-coloured head that came to our front door and then flew away!" Olive had quickly worked out that the cloak looked like the crow's wings and that the cap was its head that she saw from her window.

"Well deduced, Olive. Yes, it was me!" Ahab conceded. "They belonged to dear old Professor Peregrine Greylag. Bless his soul! Being the eccentric he was, he'd ride around this huge estate wearing his old cap and gown on his treasured pushbike. He found it the best way to get around its hundreds of acres and to keep his eccentric memory going. He was amazingly sprightly and sharp-minded for an octogenarian, I'll tell you!" He paused in reflection. "I hope I didn't startle you?" he added concernedly.

"No, not startled. It was just me that saw you, Ahab," Olive reassured him. "I was kind of bemused and amused at the same time," she replied before turning to her parents and with a loud whisper, "See, I wasn't making it up!"

Libby and Toby jointly raised their hands with an apologetic gesture to their daughter. "Sorry, Olive," they whispered resignedly as one. "We should have believed you."

"I like what you did there, Olive," said Ahab. "'Bemused and amused'! Very clever! You are a poet and you didn't know it!" They all laughed together. He suddenly refocused and changed to a more serious and thoughtful expression, before taking a deep breath, adding, "And now we get to the nitty-gritty. Have you met your new landlord yet, by the way—Tarquini Scumbali, Lord of Didsvale Manor?"

"No, we haven't," replied Libby. "We arranged everything through the local rental agent. They said he would be nice and fair to deal with though."

"Mmmmmmm... I must warn you. Oh, yes, he's nice. Very nice! Nice as pie! A pie that burns your mouth and the whole of your stomach when you don't realise how dangerously hot it is and when you expect to enjoy its taste and satisfy your belly..." replied Ahab in a very stern and serious way. "Beware of that individual. Just keep on his good side. I know more about Scumbali that you'd care to know about, trust me." Ahab came quickly out of his serious state and apologised. "Oh, I'm sorry about that. Where were we? Oh yes! So, Peregrine kindly stepped in and offered me free accommodation here in this cosy ranger's cabin, where I've made myself quite at home as you can see! Incidentally, it was he who invented that clever sonar idea to open the gate."

Olive scrambled back up onto her chair once again to re-join the others. "Well. I suppose you're wondering why I've invited you all here to Didsvale Park today as my special guests?"

"We didn't really know we were special guests until we saw the cancellation notice at the park entrance, but thank you," replied Toby appreciatively.

"And that's why it's special, and extremely secret," added Ahab intriguingly. He continued. "What I'm about to tell you is the most secret of secrets!" he said with added bemusing conviction. "Are you all sitting comfortably?" asked the captain.

"Yes, thank you," Libby responded gratefully on behalf of

all three sitting on their lofty perches.

"Then let me begin bluntly, if I may—You are here because…" He hesitated for a few seconds to stare at all three from side to side before continuing slowly and deliberately… "You are here because… I need you to look after the park while I'm away for a short while!"

Toby acted as spokesperson. "Look after the park—but how? We have no experience in park-keeping and you hardly know us."

"But I do know you now, don't I!" he said surprisingly. "You are the perfect candidates for the job. The future of this park depends on its upkeep and management just for this short time. I know you can do it. The future of this park depends on you. Please. Please!"

"No pressure then!" whispered Toby to Libby.

# Chapter 5
## *The Story of Professor Peregrine Greylag*

A few minutes of complete silence passed by before Ahab cleared his throat and went on... "Let me explain... Firstly, I need to tell you the story of the wonderful Professor Greylag, Didsvale Park's generous benefactor, whom I mentioned before. This wonderful individual kept this place going against all odds after a gentleman's agreement was made with the new estate owner. After many broken promises the professor wound up using his own money to maintain everything. However, when this money ran out he was forced to sell many of his treasured possessions to continue the maintenance of the park. This included sacrificing his fabulous miniature railway, which ran from the park, across the river bridge into the reserve, then around the manor and back again in a figure of eight. It used to attract regular visitors until it was abandoned because of lack of funds."

"Yes. I noticed a piece of track in the undergrowth when we came in," jumped in Toby.

Ahab continued. "As you have already witnessed, his splendid gardens also deteriorated into sad disarray. Sadly, we lost the professor several months ago as the result of a fateful accident on his trusty old bike within the grounds by the mighty giant oak tree."

"That must have must been who the bouquet had been left for then?" Libby asked sensitively. "We didn't read it out of privacy," she added sympathetically.

"That was very decent of you. Yes," replied Ahab with a resigned sigh before adding thoughtfully, "How he managed to lose control of his bike that way after he rode around the park and reserve on it day after day I'll never know. Seemed more than an unfortunate accident to me."

"What do you mean, Ahab, 'more than an unfortunate accident?' Who would do such a thing to the park's main benefactor, and why!" Toby added inquisitively.

"Something doesn't quite add up in my mind. Let's just call it sailor's intuition and leave it there, if you don't mind, please!" Ahab concluded, raising his hand indicating a polite stop sign.

Toby turned to Libby with an intrigued expression.

Olive tactfully broke the awkward silence that followed. "It looked like a lovely bouquet of remembrance flowers for Professor Greylag, Ahab."

"Thank you, Olive. It was the least I could do."

"I thought it might be you who left them when you appeared from that direction to surprise us," she added.

There was a long pause. Toby, Libby and Olive looked across at each other, waiting for Ahab to continue before he smiled back silently and broke away from his sadness. "Which is why everywhere is in such a mess," he stated. "I try my best but sometimes my best isn't good enough. I just can't keep up," he added resignedly. "That Lord Scumbali made all his ground staff redundant to cut cost, supposedly to pay for the repair work to be carried out. Unfortunately, it was them who always gave Peregrine an hour or two of their personal time to help."

From this point onwards, the Adamson family were mesmerised and enthralled by what they heard from Captain Ahab. Libby and Toby sat perfectly still on their chairs while Olive wormed around to get comfortable with her feet dangling around, as the story continued.

Ahab suddenly lost his friendly eccentricity and took on a more serious expression as he began to tell more of his story…

"Shortly before he passed away, Professor Greylag looked very troubled about something and suddenly took me into his confidence to share his personal secrets with me. This is what he told me." Before pausing for a few seconds and taking a deep breath for composure, he continued to elaborate. "My great friend Peregrine, that was how he liked me to call him, was a child genius. The Secret Services were always on the look-out for exceptionally gifted prodigies with genius skills and talents. His junior school headmaster pointed out that one of their pupils might be of interest to them for top-secret government work just after World War Two. He was examined and found to have an IQ above anything they had ever seen from an adult, let alone a nine-year-old boy. He was then taken to a top-secret, code-breaking facility in the Scottish Highlands, where he was well cared for and given excellent accommodation and education with other gifted children of similar ages. His parents understood how important it was to allow him to go, with a combination of great sadness and personal pride. Unfortunately, they could only tell their neighbours that he had gone into a boarding school to help with his so-called 'learning difficulties'. Unfortunately, his parents were tragically killed together in a car accident shortly after the war, leaving him orphaned. However, by an exceptional twist of fate, the childless Lord and Lady Didsvale subsequently adopted him and took him back to Didsvale Manor. When his new found doting adopted parents passed away, firstly his mother followed quickly by his father, the now adult and independent Peregrine inherited the title of Lord Didsvale of Didsvale Manor. During this time, he used his exceptional intelligence to become a renowned inventor, chemical scientist, and explorer. And that's pretty much the early story of Professor Peregrine Greylag," he concluded before taking a further deep inward breath and continuing. "However, well over two years ago now, he suddenly and surprisingly sold the manor with its estate to a new owner, the aforementioned Tarquini Scumbali! Prior to the new owner taking up residence, a surveying company had written to Peregrine claiming that the manor was deemed unsecure due to some newly discovered ancient mine workings, and therefore in desperate need of expensive support strengthening within the foundations. They showed him charts of where potential sinkholes were threatening to appear throughout the park, and needed filling in at great cost. Something didn't feel quite right about it to me," Ahab surmised.

Toby interjected confidentially. "Yes, Ahab, it's called underpinning."

"Ah yes, Toby, that was it. Underpinning! I'm not surprised you know the terminology with your background. That was definitely the word Peregrine said to me. However, I never heard of any ancient mine-workings being talked about in these parts. Underpinning! Codswallop. The biggest wallop of cods I've ever seen in all my life in every ocean!" the captain stated angrily. "Anyhow, Peregrine was shown the surveyor's evidence with some professional charts and so decided to take the only course of action available to him. There was no way he could ever afford these expensive repairs, which is how he came to put the manor and park up for sale. Then, from out of nowhere, came an offer from Mister Scumbali to buy it, promising all the funds necessary to carry out the repair work and save Didsvale Manor and the Park. All of the villagers treated him like a hero but I know the other side of that rascal. I wouldn't trust him as far as I could throw a mackerel back into the sea. And I hold the world record for mackerel throwing you know, Olive?" Ahab made the last exaggerated statement to take some of the anger out of his demeanour and to get a rewarding smile, which Olive duly provided.

Ahab recommenced. "The three conditions of the purchase agreement were that Didsvale Park ownership was to be retained by Peregrine; the manor title was to be formally granted to the new owner and Peregrine could have any one of the artefacts from within the manor house as a goodwill gesture memento. He chose his father's cherished mini pipe organ. I'll tell you more about this later. So, to that effect, Tarquini Scumbali became the new Lord Didsvale and dear old Peregrine was more than happy to be known simply as Professor Greylag—something that he was quite proud and happy to be referred to, as it happened. He led a quiet life in the old engine shed office, which became his living accommodation, on what was now his new estate. The small amount of money received from the sale of the manor was with what Peregrine used to keep the park open with access to the nature reserve, for as long as Tarquini Scumbali permitted. By 'permitted' this meant that it wasn't a legal agreement and for that reason, he had Peregrine emotionally blackmailed, fearing that one day the reserve could be severed from the park. There's another thing. "Strangely, since Scumbali moved in, there have been two huge commercial lorries parked behind the manor house, but I haven't seen any workers around or any work being visibly done around the manor house. He's now put warning signs up all around the entire estate boundaries and the nature reserve, saying 'KEEP OUT—DANGER— SINKHOLES' to scare anyone off!"

"Yes. We saw one on the other side of the river on our way in," Toby pointed out.

"That's correct," said Ahab. "The course of the River Babble is the original boundary between the reserve and the park, before the old Lord and Lady Greylag bought the park for its long-term protection and included it into their estate. It's the reserve that Scumbali is most secretive about though," he added thoughtfully.

Libby leapt in with a question. "This Tarquini Scumbali, or Lord Scumbali as he's now known. Why didn't he offer Kingfisher Cottage to Peregrine when he bought the estate from him?"

"Why indeed not, Libby! Why indeed not!" replied Ahab. "Perhaps Lord 'Scumbags' had a reason for him not to be too close to the Manor. Perhaps there was something that he wanted to keep secret! When the Adamson family applied to rent Kingfisher Cottage, it provided him with the perfect public relations opportunity. As long as he keeps you sweet, you'll paint a very nice picture of him in the village." He paused. "Tell me. Has he asked you for much rent so far?"

Toby stepped in thoughtfully. "Actually, as you happen to mention it, he's provided it free for the first three months."

"How kind and considerate," said Ahab, sarcastically.

Toby, Libby and Olive looked deep in thought, trying to make sense out of Ahab's astounding words, before Toby stepped in. "Please tell us more about Professor Peregrine Greylag and his secret school. Please!" he begged further.

Ahab took up the request. "Of course, Toby. Now this sounds incredulous and farfetched, but every single word is true." He took in a deep breath before continuing. "Amongst the top secret research that Peregrine worked on in the Scottish Highlands was a programme based on the way pigeons were trained to take secret messages beyond enemy lines and then guide them safely back home. You may have heard about this in those wartime stories. After Peregrine was adopted and brought to Didsvale Manor, he developed a keen interest in birdlife by watching and studying their behaviours avidly across the park from his bedroom window. Then, by using what he'd recorded, worked tirelessly creating various amazing theories. As soon as he arrived in the Scottish Highlands, he continued to work on his theories in his spare evening time. So, here's the exciting part. Hang on tight!" The three entranced listeners leant a little further forward to catch every word. The captain pressed on with his story... "Using the success that he had with the secret wartime pigeons and other bird species, he worked tirelessly alone in his bedroom every evening to work on 'Project Smew' as he named it. Peregrine had a theory that all birds received magnetic brainwaves on a special frequency that could be encrypted and translated into a new kind of global communication formula." He asked Toby, Libby and Olive, "If you think about it? Have you ever wondered why you see birds flying in all directions, here there and everywhere, for seemingly no apparent reason, not just to gather food but just randomly flying about? Ever thought why that is? Why is it that you see ducks flying around in panic as if they didn't want to be up there in the first place?"

The three shrugged their shoulders as Libby self-questioned in reply. "Do you know? I'd never given that a second thought till you mentioned it! But they do all seem to be flying here there and everywhere with no absolute purpose. As if they are all…" then before she could finish his sentence, Ahab interrupted to complete her sentence, "… as if they were all responding to some kind of navigational communication signals that were proving coordinates to direct them somehow. Yes, precisely!" he confirmed back to her.

"And so, Peregrine discovered that this 'flying phenomenon' as you put it was for a very important reason. That was to ensure that all birds from around the world get into precise positions to receive birdbrain signals from other birds so they can navigate them to and from anywhere in the world. Something we familiarly call migration! Peregrine had amazingly tapped into this avian electronic messaging phenomenon. And! Not only did he discover this within the world's bird family, but he also told me about some other top-secret research he was carrying out by somehow utilising similar frequencies by intercepting human thought signals and converting them into a parallel frequency. Peregrine did some more research, saying he was working to discover this undiscovered frequency, which could convey happy memory thoughts from the past into present day reality, as he described it to me! He used to say, in simple terms, that if around sixty per cent or more of the human body is made up of water, then it was more than likely that all signals such as thought signals, radio signals, TV signals, phone signals and the like, are passing through our brains and bodies all of the time. It was just a question of separating the human signals from the birdbrain signals and hey presto, he would have his new discovery! He said he was close to discovering how to summon these happy memories from the past with the same technology. He had a theory that déjà vu, second-sight and ESP, were all part of that same science just waiting to be discovered, and the explanation for what's commonly known as 'sixth sense'! So, effectively, someone could go back to a point in time and experience it in reality. He said this was possible by coating an old cherished photograph in magicmunchymulch and processing it through this weird new invention of his. He was convinced he could somehow bring old cherished photographs back to life. He said he was on the verge of discovering something called 'photo...'" He looked upwards, searching for the rest of the word in his mind before finishing proudly. "...thinky! That was it, photothinky as he called it! Not easy for me to remember a complicated word like that one!" he confessed. "Anyway, he had a quirky name for this project. He called it his Silver Dream Machine project."

Olive quickly shot her hand up in the air and interjected. "Excuse me, Captain Ahab. Can you tell me what a brainwave is and the other stuff you mentioned just then?"

"Well, that's an easy one, Olive," replied the captain. And just for Olive's entertainment, he embellished the story a little more. "To keep it simple, young Olive! You know when a brilliant idea comes into your head from nowhere? Like a big light bulb being switched on in your head and sort of lights up your brain?"

Olive screwed her face up in thought before recognising

what he meant. "Yeah! I get them all the time," she answered interestedly.

"Well, that's a brainwave! And do you know where all the bird brainwaves went to, according to the wonderful Professor Peregrine Greylag?" he asked further. Olive shook her head nonplussed. "They go to the global magnetic brainwave deep blue vortex!" exclaimed Ahab. Olive sat with mouth agape. "Yes, even birds have brains. Especially the crow family, who have some of the brainiest bird brainboxes of the bird world, I may have you know! And Olive? Just imagine being able to communicate with every birdbrain on this planet! The other human phenomenon you asked about, Olive! Well, second sight and déjà vu are that feeling that for a few seconds you are convinced to have lived through a present experience before. It translates into English from French as 'already seen'. Sixth sense and extra sensory perception is when information is gathered by another unknown sense. Second sight is the supposed ability to predict the future, and extrasensory perception, or ESP as it's commonly called, is when you experience a million-to-one, unexplained coincidence, such as when you think of a friend who you've not seen for ages. No sooner have you thought of that person, than the doorbell rings and there they are coming to visit you, large as life. That's no coincidence! It was meant to happen. A photographic memory is an amazing gift that a very small number of humans have. It enables them to look at something and record the image in their magnetic memory in every minute detail. They're then able to recall that memory and those details at any given time."

Ahab took a deep inward breath on completing his lecture to Olive, whose facial expression of deep, thoughtful concentration stayed firmly in place as she asked, "You mean to say that ESP is like when I saw writing in the sky written by starlings. Were they responding to birdbrain brainwave signals?" she asked enthusiastically.

Ahab leant backwards in his chair with shock and surprise. He looked sideways at Libby and Toby for confirmation of Olive's personal account before slowly leaning forwards again and replying. "And when exactly did this happen, Olive?" he queried.

Libby jumped in before Olive could respond. "Oh, we'd had a tiring day and she'd had a dream during her cat nap! She was exhausted after a long day."

Olive looked back disgruntled at her mother before turning to Ahab. "It wasn't a dream, Captain Ahab. It was real! Honestly! The starlings wrote *Libby Toby Olive*... And then... *Welcome to Kingfisher Cottage.* How do you explain that? Dad told me it was called a murmuration made up of hundreds of thousands of starlings," her voice panting in hurried excitement.

Ahab's eyes looked around the room as if he was lost in the content of Olive's revelation, before training his eyes back onto each of the three fascinated listeners. "Perhaps it had something to do with Peregrine's research!" he revealed eerily.

"See!" Olive gloated to her sceptical parents.

"Let's not jump to conclusions yet, though. All will be revealed in the fullness of time," said Ahab, with a philosophical attempt to quell Olive's excitement and at the same time aiming to pacify her parents. "So, in simple terms, Peregrine was originally working on capturing, deciphering and processing all of this information with his invention, like a global satellite dish that all the birds of the world would use to communicate and navigate by. He did this by selecting one of the most suitable trees in the park that closest resembled the mythical Oakeycokey tree of Pamona Atoll found in the unchartered waters of the Bermuda Triangle. He used this tree and its leaves as his antenna mast to intercept and capture those waves travelling to the global magnetic brainwave deep blue vortex on the atoll."

"Excuse me, Ahab." Olive shot her hand up to ask another question. "What's the Oakeycokey tree?"

"Oh—so sorry—I'm going too fast for us all, aren't I? I'll come back to that bit again soon."

The captain continued his story. "For simplicity, he called his new global bird language 'Squawkerlingo'! How funny was that!" he emphasised loudly while gaining full agreement from all three, fascinated with open mouths and nodding heads. "So, the **'SMEW'** part of the project really stands for *Squawkerlingo! Migration! Encryption! Worldwide!* Or his 'squawkbox', as the professor lovingly named his splendid invention. So, he had a great sense of humour as you can see. He now had the mainframe for SMEW but it was missing one major lacked component, he said…" Ahab then made a slight sighing pause before concluding, "…the means to bring his invention to life!" he added excitedly. "Just hold onto those thoughts for one little while," Ahab urged to the enthralled Adamsons as he fiddled with his cap with nervous excitement. "Yesterday, this arrived." He dragged out a small box from underneath his seat. "It arrived by special courier, addressed to me personally. When I opened it I found this solicitor's letter along with these items inside. It simply read… '*To Captain Ahab McCrab—my great trusted friend and seafarer of all seafarers. In the event that I depart this world before you do, I bequeath these personal items to you for safekeeping—*

*Remember! Unlock the oceans of your mind, seek and you shall find...! Your dear friend, Professor Peregrine Greylag.'* In the box I found his treasured old school cap and university cloak. I also found these three keys contained in a small cloth bag; each one is connected to a leather cord and individually labelled in the professor's own handwriting like this—'*Engine Shed, Writing Desk and Telescope*'. Ahab proceeded to show them the labels one by one... *Engine Shed* written on the first, followed by *Writing Desk* on the second and *Telescope* on the last. "There's a different inscription on each one as well," he explained, before pondering a little. The professor told me once that his telescope was an antique family heirloom from the family's nautical past centuries ago. I would often see him bird watching with it. Not the ideal means to do his twitching with, but that was dear old Peregrine, unconventional to the end! He was always seen it with it around his neck, but strangely missing at the time of his accident! He must have put it in a safe place for some reason. Unfortunately, his cherished old bike was wrecked during the accident, but I rescued it and lovingly repaired it. As a tribute to his memory, I now ride it myself around the park. I'm sure he wouldn't have minded me doing that. Would he?" asking the Adamsons to support his decision.

"No, no. Not all," they all agreed, nodding sympathetically in unison.

"Well, let's get to the nub of the matter. Before I go away, I would like for you all to take ownership of these keys and make good use of them. It's what Peregrine would have appreciated, and particularly if he knew what good homes they were going to," he said with a knowing smile. "So firstly!" he announced while focussing his piercing sea green eyes onto

Olive. "Olive, I would like you to take care of his old writing desk. Maybe you'd like to write some of your wonderful stories on it," he asked the astounded recipient while dangling the key labelled '*Writing Desk*'tantalisingly in front of her.

"Really!" Olive answered aghast with surprise. "Well, *yes,* absolutely, Captain Ahab. Thank you," she added excitedly as she grasped the key and read its label out aloud. *"Writing Desk,"* before turning it over to read out the inscription. *"Seek and you shall find —!"* Mmmm. I wonder what this means? she thought to herself. "Are you sure that the professor would have wanted me to have this?"

"On the contrary. He'd be absolutely overjoyed to know it's gone to such a talented young writer," Ahab added flatteringly.

"Wow, thanks, Ahab. I'll take extra care of it!" replied Olive, thrilled by the response.

"There is one extra condition though…" Ahab added intriguingly. Olive glanced back at Ahab with concerned anticipation. "…which is that I get to read the first story you write on it?" he asked, with a warm sparkle in his eyes.

"No problem. It's a promise," Olive replied confidently, while draping the shiny new possession safely around her neck.

The captain turned to Toby. "And this one's for you," stretching out his arm.

Toby's eyes opened large with anticipation as he grasped the second key and read the label out loud. "'*Engine Shed*'! Wow, thank you, Ahab. I'm deeply honoured." He too turned over his label and read out the inscription aloud. "'*Appearances Deceive!*' I wonder what that means," he mused to himself.

"Oh, don't thank me, thank the professor," Ahab humbly replied. "If he knew that such a keen railway enthusiast and gifted engineer as you would be safeguarding it, I think he'd be honoured himself!"

"I'm flattered, Ahab. I'll guard it with my life," Toby commented as he glared mysteriously at his key.

He then turned to Libby. "And last, but not least, Libby. This one's for you," said Ahab as he offered her the third key from his hand. "It's like handing out medals at the Olympics, isn't it! Except in this case, you're all winners!" he added with a broad smile. Libby extended her cupped hands, into which Ahab dropped the last key. "And this is the special *'Telescope'* key for you to look after, and one of the professor's most treasured possessions. I do hope you find it." She turned over her label to read the wording *'Keep your eye on the Prize!'* How very strange and cryptic, she thought.

"Wow. I'll treasure it also. Don't worry about that," she added reassuringly. "Are you really sure, Ahab?" Libby emphasised with astonishment as she carefully took the last key and hung it safely around her neck. "But it was the professor's family heirloom and probably very valuable."

"But nothing will be more valuable than what you see through that telescope. You'll be seeing all that wildlife on behalf of its previous owner," Ahab reasoned. "All of the wonderful nature within the park and on the river that the professor used to enjoy. Perhaps you can produce a book about the park one day and fill it with your wonderful drawings."

"I'd absolutely love that. Thanks, Ahab. Certainly, I'll take care of it almost as though the professor is still looking through it!"

"Very good," he replied with a warm smile. "So, it's

extremely important that you do whatever is necessary with these keys Peregrine has left, and help to maintain the park for me during my short absence. I've never been in the train shed myself. It was where Peregrine spent most of his time, working on his secret projects and trying to restore his beloved Flying Cootsman steam engine in the hope that one day he would have it up and running again. It was out of bounds to anyone else bar him."

"Can you tell us more about his miniature railway and train engine shed please, Ahab," Toby enquired with a great deal of enthusiasm.

"Absolutely," replied the captain. "Well, the previous owners of the Didsvale Manor and its estate, Lord and Lady Greylag, doted on their newly adopted son, Peregrine, and supported him in every way they could. One day, Lord Didsvale asked Peregrine what his ideal dream was if he could accomplish it himself. The old Lord Didsvale was no intellectual slouch himself and in fact, a talented musician. He was even the voluntary church organist you know!" Being the passionate musician he was, you could often hear the stirring sound of him playing far into the estate grounds from inside the manor when the windows were wide open. It was the old mini pipe organ from Didsvale Church that had been replaced with a brand-new grander version. This being due to his generosity in providing most of the purchase funds. I digress! Anyhow, Peregrine's answer to his father's challenging question was his ambition to build a miniature train railway around the whole estate for the local villagers and their families to enjoy. Peregrine was an absolute railway nut as well as a very keen birdwatcher. With the help of some estate workers, he successfully laid miles and miles of track running in a loop from the park entrance and over a bridge into the manor house estate, into the nature reserve and then back to the park entrance again. He built stations every so often for passengers to hop on and off wherever and whenever they wanted to. There was '**Didsvale Park Station**', by the park entrance, which was the main terminus and had a souvenir shop and tearoom for the visitors, followed by '**Mighty Oak Tree Station**', '**Bosun's Cabin Halt**', '**River Babble Bridge Station**', '**Didsvale Manor Station**', '**Nature Reserve Lake Station**' and '**Didsvale Manor Station**', before returning back again to Didsvale Park Station. Lord Didsvale generously invested in three brand new miniature steam train engines for the young Peregrine to indulge in to organise and manage fund raising rides around the park. He would have a couple of engines running at any one time per day. They were just about big enough for two adults to sit in its open driver's cab able to operate it, and were several metres in length. They were built to run along a narrow track, which didn't take up much space, leaving plenty of room for people to walk or cycle alongside so they could explore other parts of the park. Peregrine named the engines after some of his favourite birds from the reserve. He called them Bullfinch, Nuthatch, and Sparrow Hawk. As a challenge to Peregrine's engineering prowess, Lord Greylag snapped up a dilapidated old train engine, which he had found condemned in a scrap yard and cost next to nothing for him to purchase. It was in such a state that I remember Peregrine saying that the scrap yard almost wanted to pay his father for the trouble of taking it away! So, this was the engineering project challenge that Lord Didsvale gave to Peregrine. In keeping with his sense of humour, Peregrine decided to name it the '*Flying Cootsman*', after his favourite water fowl, the coot, that he watched every day on the river that flows through the estate!"

Toby laughed out loud. "I get it. That's hilarious, Ahab. The Flying Cootsman! That's a really clever twist of the name of the world-famous steam train. I love it!" he stated keenly.

"Along with the three steam engines," Ahab continued, "Lord Greylag bought four open-sided miniature train carriages that could snugly seat any passenger safely on board for each trip. The carriages were connected to whichever engine was being used on any particular day. Well, after his parents had passed away, Peregrine built himself a circular brick building with a wooden roof as a workshop and shed for these steam engines' safe storage. He situated it discreetly and well out of the way from the public's gaze at the far end of the park. He rambled on to me once saying something about it being on the site of some kind of fabled mysterious tree. Anyway, that was the last he spoke about it. However, when you hear the rest of this tale, maybe it'll make more sense. I'll tell you what though, he spent almost every minute of his spare time locked in that engine shed and kept anyone else from stepping inside. It's an absolute privilege that you now have the key to it!" Ahab refocused back to where he left off, with an apology to his deeply engaged audience. "Peregrine once told me that he'd moved from his nearby lodgings and now made it his home, and it came in very handy when he worked well into the night. He explained to me one day that, historically, this type of railway building was originally called a 'roundhouse' and quite familiar back in the day. Ahab turned his attention to Olive. "Basically Olive, a roundhouse is what it says on the can. It's a circular shaped building able to store all the engines around a central revolving turntable. It has a

56

large air vent on the roof to allow any engine smoke and steam out. When Peregrine wanted an engine for the day, it was moved from one of several positions around the turntable. To get an engine into the shed it was driven onto the turntable and then rotated until it lined up with a vacant storage position, and for getting out of the shed it was driven back onto the turntable and then lined up with the exit track to be driven outside, where it would be coupled up to the four passenger carriages ready for the day's visitors. So there you are—that's a roundhouse for you—a very simple and effective way of swapping each train around and facing it the right way without any inconvenience to the other engines, and keeping your engines maintained in good working condition under a weather protective roof."

"Yes, you used to see them all over the country many years ago in the days of steam railways." Toby jumped in to reminisce.

Olive then raised a hand to make her own inquisitive contribution. "Excuse me, Ahab. Was it something like my compass with different points? Mum showed me how to use a compass. Didn't you, Mum?"

Libby nodded in agreement. "Yes. I see exactly where you're coming from, Olive. Well done!"

Ahab responded thoughtfully. "I've never really considered that, Olive. But yes! That's a very good comparison. Who knows what you'll find in that engine shed, but I'll tell you what, it's a real privilege that you're all able to go in there. All will be revealed in the fullness of time!" he added wisely again before continuing. "Anyway, we must move on. The train rides and facilities at Didsvale Station provided quite a lot of income towards the upkeep of the park, ever since Peregrine sold the estate to Tarquini Scumbali. Eventually though, he had to sell off all the working engines to keep the park financially operational until the only engine left was the Flying Cootsman, which he just about manages to refurbish in time and took her on her maiden trip, which was quite a celebration I can tell you! Unfortunately, the miniature railway trips had to be sacrificed due to lack of funds. Not only that, but the track was gradually swallowed up in the undergrowth due lack of funds. As for the carriages, he kept those to gradually break up as firewood to feed his wood burner and keep him warm during the winter months. So sad! However, on the plus side and being the determined engineer he was, Peregrine worked day and night on maintaining the Flying Cootsman to full working condition so she would be running round the park in full steam one day. Yes. Like a man possessed, his ambition was that he could renovate the railway for the benefit of the villagers again. Not only did he confide in me that he was spending all that time in the engine shed maintaining the Flying Cootsman, but he was also working on his top secret 'SMEW' machine!

"Ah yes," Ahab mused. "The professor used to spend nearly every minute of his time locked away in that engine room, desperately trying to restore the engine when he wasn't tending to the park. It was fast becoming a losing battle. As part of the original hand-over conditions with Tarquini Scumbali, he wasn't allowed to ask for voluntary help from the villagers because of insurance restrictions."

"What a rotter he sounds like!" snapped Toby with anger. "So that's what I tripped over when we entered the park! It was a piece of the old Lord Greylag's overgrown railway track," he added, with a certain amount of smug self-satisfaction to the others.

"We're sorry to interrupt you, Ahab," Libby apologised. "Please go on," she begged.

"So, poor old Flying Cootsman hasn't seen life in her old boiler since the accident and she never met Peregrine's ambition to have her running on his beloved railway again," he added sadly.

Ahab then turned his attention over to Toby. "So, that's why you have the roundhouse engine shed key, Toby. With your engineering skill, maybe you can tinker around and maybe bring Peregrine's prized possession back to life again?"

Toby looked exasperated. "Really, Ahab? I'm flattered. Well, thank you very much. I'll certainly give it my best shot," he replied.

"But I digress. Here's the main reason why I am desperately seeking your help and confiding with you all this way. To continue, I must ask you all that you do not disclose to another living soul what I am about to share with you. Please keep your minds and imaginations as open as you can. Are you ready?" Ahab asked the three listeners, who then nodded vigorously in agreement. "This is the story I was told by the professor , which I ask you to believe. You must believe E...V... E... R... Y... single word!" he spelt out letter by letter to the Adamsons, rigidly alert to the impending story.

Captain Ahab then continued with his story, wearing the most serious of expressions. His eyes scanned back and forth across each of the three trance-like faces to gain maximum attention and concentration… "OK. Here we go… After he left the top-secret facility in the Scottish Highlands as a young child, the professor continued working on his SMEW research for some time. As I mentioned, he was convinced that somewhere within the Bermuda Triangle existed a location where all bird brainwave transmissions converged, before disappearing into a phenomenon he described as the deep blue brainwave vortex. He was obsessed with trying to locate and study this phenomenon. With his mathematical genius, he was able to set his compass to a direction that no other living soul had ever found. He called it 'south by south west recurring', or 'the fifth direction'. Maybe you know what this conundrum might mean?" he asked the enthralled listeners. "I didn't quite understand the professor's weird theory, but it had something to do with the circumference of a circle and a number of **pies** making a formula, then taking that same number of **pies** and applying it to directions around the circumference of a compass. Apparently, you can never have a full **pie**, even until the end of time! He then took this same **pie** formula of his and mixed it into some kind of equator." He quickly corrected himself. "Hang on a second. I think that should be **equation**! Sorry! So, he mashed all this gibberish scientific stuff up with the directions of a compass and discovered a new direction that would take him to places that no human had ever visited. In all my seafaring days, I never heard of anything so bizarre. However, knowing the professor as I did, something told me to trust in whatever he was saying as he always asked me to do. Does that make sense to you?" He looked around at the faces of the Adamsons, all displaying the same mixture of confused and bewildered expressions.

Then Olive shot her hand up, awaiting Captain Ahab's response. "Yes, my dear?" he replied.

"I may know what Professor Greylag meant. We did it at school." She looked at her parents for support in explaining to Ahab the real meaning of his description without offending his

60

intelligence. They all responded with wry smiles and nods to carry on. She began to speak, with her face strained with concentration. "I think this is what he was trying to explain to you, Captain Ahab. The **pies**, which Professor Greylag described to you, is how a circle is measured and is known as **Pi**, spelt **P.i.**," she emphasised. "Then the professor took this different geometric kind of **Pi**, and knowing that it would never ever divide exactly into the circumference of a circle and would go on to infinity. He created a new '**equation**' by combining this with all the various compass points and found the missing direction that he explained to you as 'south by south west recurring'. **Recurring** means to go on for infinity! Forever! It sounds to me like the professor discovered a completely new compass direction that shouldn't exist but does. She pursed her lips and furrowed her brow in thought before concluding. "Well, at least that's what I think!" she ended, with a satisfied expression to herself.

Ahab had sat transfixed on Olive as she made her interpretation to him, until he recovered his composure to agree without losing face. "Exactly, Olive. Just as you say!" He then continued. "So, his work could only be completed if he were able to find this phenomenon and somehow bring his findings back to Didsvale for further research. He made lengthy preparations before finally setting sail on his sailboat, 'Pretty Pol', from Didsvale Ferry landing." The captain stopped speaking for a second and looked directly at Olive. "And why did he embark on a sailboat instead of something more powerful, you may ask yourself?"

Olive looked straight back, stumped by the question. "I've no idea, Captain Ahab. Why?"

"Why, Olive?" Ahab teased with over-stated

astonishment. "The answer's as plain as the nose on your face! Because if he had any other noises, like from an engine or radio, they may have interfered with the south by south west recurring direction frequency. The only sound permitted was the sound of the wind and the waves."

Olive responded with a look of gratitude.

Ahab continued. "After many months sailing towards South by South-West recurring, the Professor eventually crossed the mysterious Sargasso Sea before entering the uncharted gateway into the Bermuda Triangle and beyond. The evening sky took on a completely different appearance at his new found location that bore no resemblance whatsoever to the galaxy that he had so much knowledge of and had brought him to the very edge of his destination. As daylight broke once again, and believing he was lost in the windless ocean and never able to reach his fabled Island due to exhaustion, the sunshine above was suddenly blotted out by an enormous shadow. His sails began to billow with wind from the massive flapping wings of the largest bird he had ever seen. He was then swept along for another night by what turned out to be a gigantic albatross, before making landfall on a tiny atoll island which he later began to explore. As he made his way across the island, he encountered the most peculiar species of parrot that he had ever seen with a blue and iridescent yellowy-orange coloured body with blue striped plumage. It was perched on a branch of the oddest looking tree he'd ever seen! It would have looked quite at home in one of Picasso's brightly colourful abstract paintings! The strange looking Parrot suddenly *spoke* to the professor and introduced himself as Methuselah the Mighty Macaw of Pamona Atoll. He went on to explain that the island was called Pamona Atoll after the mythical goddess of fruitful abundance and that this wasn't a myth at all but pure reality! The strange parrot told the professor that he had been expecting him because the professor's very own, uniquely incredible, brainwaves had been detected after they were collected within the leaves of the island's only tree, before entering the brainwave blue hole vortex deep within the giant tree trunk's roots within a massive underground labyrinth. The island's tree was called the 'Deep Blue Brainwave Vortex Tree' and Methuselah explained that he knew it was only a matter of time before fate delivered Professor Greylag to the island, after being guided there under the safe wings of Argyll the Albatross, as he was known. Upon seeing this weird looking tree for the first time, the professor was amazed how much it reminded him of the Mighty Oak tree back home here in the park, which he called his Oakeycokey Tree. You see this was because of the similarly long branches like human arms and legs that danced in the breeze. He found later that when he sang the Hokey Cokey song back home in Didsvale Park near the tree he noticed that the squibrels would join in word for word, note for note. They would then perform this for the park visitors. It went like this…" at which point, Captain Ahab looked at Olive with a wide smile and began to sing some of the opening lyrics to the song, very slowly and softly…

" *'You put your left arm in, your left arm out. In, out, in, out, you shake it all about.*
*You do the Hokey Cokey and you turn around. That's what it's all about…'*
…That one!" he declared with an apologetic wave of his hand after descending into an awkward rambling hum as he

forgot the remaining lyrics.

Olive jumped in keenly. "We know, Ahab. That was another of the songs we heard at the giant tree when we walked across the park. Yes. REAL songs!" she emphasised to her parents.

Ahab picked up where he'd forgetfully left off, "…and the tree's multi-coloured leaves swayed like an extravagant carnival costume, is how the professor described it! Well, that was before he realised there was no breeze around and something else was disturbing the tree, completely camouflaged against it. Methuselah explained that this single tree was home to small native creatures called the Younoseeme Squibrels, or to use their scientific name, which is, 'SupercamouflagiousPomonaSquibrelimulchyotious'.

"It was they who made the tree dance so entertainingly as they scampered around from branch to branch. Apparently, they are a distant relative to our very own native red squirrels, he went on to say. Methuselah the Mighty Macaw also explained that this unique tree produced a special fruit with seeds like acorn seeds, except these seeds contained a unique juice with magical properties. The professor was told that this juice was sprinkled on fallen leaves from the 'Deep Blue Brainwave Vortex Tree' and then made into a soft, pulpy, squidgy substance, which was locally known as 'magicmunchymulch'. He said that the Squibrels ate this as their staple diet. Just like a panda needs eucalyptus leaves to survive! However, the most miniscule drop of juice diluted into the leaves made them enough magicmunchymulch to last for many years. When they consumed the magicmunchymulch, it made them super camouflaged to any immediate surrounding, appearing to be visible to the naked eye. Not only that,

Methuselah told him, but the magicmunchymulch also helped them to decipher all the world's 'birdbrain' signals. These are the same signals that the Deep Blue Brainwave Vortex Tree's leaves intercepted and processed into the international bird language Peregrine later aptly named Squawkerlingo! Peregrine was given permission to take two very, very special Squibrels back home with him to Didsvale Park, because they could help to interpret the secret bird language signal codes to help with his research. This was agreed, on the professor's promise that he would return them when they had exhausted their supply of juice. He affectionately called these unique creatures Stanley and Livingstone after the two famous explorers. Methuselah the Mighty Macaw also told him that the juice from the seeds had another special power when it made the magicmunchymulch. He said that this power could produce some kind of secret memory energy and that the professor would know exactly when and where it would be needed. Peregrine was then given a tiny amount of special juice droplets, which he carefully poured into his small experimental glass phial to bring safely home. Apparently, he returned to Didsvale with the help of Argyll the Albatross, which blew him all the way back home from Pamona Atoll. After his return, he spent all of his spare time, morning, noon and night, locked away in his engine shed continuing his research in complete privacy.

"You must never tell another soul, but this is what the professor whispered to me with his last words when I found him by the mighty oak tree after his terrible accident on that fateful day. It looked to me as though he had just rushed back to one of his eccentric experiments and lost control of his bike just before he got there. I reckon it was one of his experiments because I noticed four weird round marks next to the tree flattened in the grass. As he lay there, he whispered the following words to me, '*Ahab, my friend, you must go to Pamona Atoll with all haste and get more Oakeycokey juice to continue my research. I have used the very last droplets making the last batch of magicmunchymulch. It's now almost all gone. Stanley and Livingstone, the Squibrels, must return home because I gave my word to Methuselah the Mighty Macaw that I would do so. You will trust the new family coming to Kingfisher Cottage as they will help to continue my work with the little remaining magicmunchymulch until you return with a new supply. I have set up a secret alert command in Squawkerlingo for your ship's bell and this is what you must do. You must repeat these words as you ring. 'When the last of eight bells makes its ring, mighty Argyll will take to wing. He'll billow your sails and give you speed, to Pamona Atoll for the juice we need!... Pretty Pol is ready for you at the old ferry landing. Safe journey, my friend, but beware of Scumbali's deadly dro...'!*" Ahab composed himself before addressing the three transfixed figures. "Unfortunately, I didn't catch his last words as he sadly faded away." Ahab's eyes welled up and a sole tear ran down his cheek before disappearing into his fluffy beard. He pulled a blue spotted handkerchief from his waistcoat pocket, quickly dabbing his eye dry once more. "You see, my new friends! This is why I need your help. It's almost as though the professor knew you would be coming to the village to help. Maybe you can unravel this mystery in some way? I told you he had a very special mind, didn't I! As you will appreciate, I need to return to Pamona Atoll without delay. This is why I've asked for this special, special favour of you. After hearing about the professor's plight, can I rely on you all to look after the park for me for a few days while I'm away? No, not for me," he suddenly corrected himself. "I'm asking this favour in the memory of my friend and the park's wonderful benefactor, Professor Peregrine Greylag, so that we can carry on his work somehow?"

Toby and Libby looked at each other for joint reassurance, while Olive closed her eyes and crossed her fingers. Libby replied. "We'd be glad to, Ahab. And besides, you've trusted us with these keys," she added.

At which point, Olive opened her eyes once her wish had come true, and responded with an excited whisper to herself... "—Yes! Result! I'm going to be a park ranger!"

"From what the professor mysteriously said about you with his strange premonition, I have a feeling the keys are in the safest place they could ever be and with their rightful owners!" The Captain looked admiringly at the three, who all nodded with modest approval.

"We must meet here at Bosun's Cabin promptly at seven thirty in the morning before I embark from the old ferry landing down the river, so I can catch the morning tide. It'll be nice and quiet. There's one last important thing that needs to be done before my departure. As I leave Bosun's Cabin, I need someone to ring the bell. Now, who remembers the professor's rhyme?" he asked.

Toby and Libby looked at each other, murmuring random words in hope before Olive suddenly shot her arm upwards and shouted excitedly, "I know it, Captain Ahab. '*As the last of eight bells ends its ring, mighty Argyll will take to wing. He'll billow your sails and give you speed, to Pamona Island for the juice we need*'."

"Excellent, Olive. That's sorted. You can be my Ship's

Bell Officer. An extremely important post!" Ahab proclaimed. Olive looked at her parents with a combination of pride and smugness.

"I'll see you all back here at Bosun's Cabin tomorrow morning at seven thirty sharp?" he confirmed.

"All agreed!" responded the excited, but apprehensive, parents together.

They all stepped outside the cabin. Just as the Adamsons moved away, Ahab pointed towards the white rockery stones with bright blue letters painted on each individual stone spelling out the name 'Key West' shouting. "Wait! I nearly forgot something very important. If you need to get into Bosun's Cabin while I'm away, look underneath the first stone to find the key. The westerly 'K' of Key West!"

"Aye! Aye! Cap'n. Message received and understood," said Olive fondly as she turned to see Captain Ahab McCrab saluting and laughing to her from the step of Bosun's Cabin. She waved goodbye to him in return before his laughing faded into the distance.

# Chapter 6
## Scumbali Snoops on the Meeting

Over at Didsvale Manor, Tarquini Scumbali watched his mother spy drone through his remote camera. The drone was hovering almost silently just above Bosun's Cabin, where it picked up the amplified voices of the captain and his guests inside. It had arrived to pick up some of the conversation between the captain and the Adamsons in between signal disruptions caused by the surrounding trees, meaning that Scumbali had to strain his ear to catch bits of the conversation. However, it was sufficient for him to hatch his dastardly plans. "Well done indeed, mother ship of Tarquini Scumbali's Darth Drone Squadron. How interesting. How very, very interesting! So, the least I know now is that the mad professor wasn't as barmy as I thought after all! He just shouldn't have been so nosey, snooping around my study computer database and my trucks to uncover my ingenious little scheme! But with him now well out of the way after 'his very unfortunate accident', I can put my lucrative plan into action. Firstly, I need to get those numbskull nitwits on the local council to approve my wind turbine eco scheme. What they won't be aware of is my secret underground drone bunker being hidden directly beneath it! I'll soon have my massive fleet of drones whirring all around the country in the dead of night collecting the stolen property from my network of top class burglars and whirring it all back here to Didsvale Manor. All of that fake sink hole and underpinning nonsense to close the estate's nature reserve has fooled everyone. It's the ideal smoke screen that even the world's largest wind turbine can't blow away!" The crescendo of Scumbali's excitement suddenly lowered as he changed into a deep trance and went on. "So, the Adamsons have no idea what they're getting themselves into and will soon be at my disposal. It's also such a pity that my dear old madcap Dotty D'eath is sure to become a liability. What a pity. It looks as though I'll have to summon my loyal drones for yet another accident. D'eath by name and death by nature! Perhaps I can capture this mythical beast of a bird they talk about and get it to propel the sails of my wind turbine with its mythical wings. Giant Albatross? How ludicrous! While that stupid sailor man is away on the high seas, he'll be exactly where I want him— well out of the way. You are going to be my perfect alibi, precious Captain Ahab McCrab, even if you don't know it yet! Yes, Tarquini, your 'money-spinning' machine will soon be reality. '**Money-Spinning**'. How apt! Ha! Ha! Ha! Haaaaaaaa!" finished the devious Tarquini Scumbali to himself with uncontrollable evil laughter.

# Chapter 7
## Meeting Tarquini Scumbali

The Adamson family had said their collective goodbyes to Captain Ahab before making their way home after their eventful and mind-blowing trip to Didsvale Park. Olive went straight off to bed, excited at the prospect of the following day's adventure. She shouted down the stairs on the way to her bedroom, "And don't forget the promises we all made to Captain Ahab. Good night, watch the bugs don't bite and don't forget to keep your keys safe for tomorrow. I'm going to sleep with mine!"

"Goodnight, Olive," her parents replied in unison.

"Well," said Toby to Libby. "I don't know about you but I'm mentally exhausted after all that and ready for bed myself. Yes. She's right. Let's keep our keys in a safe place for tomorrow. I'm getting as excited as Olive!" he added.

"Me too!" agreed Libby. "Looks like we've got a big commitment coming up! We must go along with Captain Ahab's fantastical story," she said sceptically, "even if it's just for Olive's sake for now. Why don't we go along with it and see what happens when we go back to the park in the morning? What a storyteller he is. He nearly had me convinced for a moment. I think Captain Ahab has another special tour for us around the park. Seven thirty a.m. is an excellent time to hear the birds' dawn chorus. Perhaps it's that?"

"Perhaps," offered Toby as the two made their way to bed.

"Just make sure any magical starling murmuration dreams don't wake you up!" commented Toby humorously to Libby as he followed her upstairs.

The Adamsons were up and about the following morning at five a.m. to allow them sufficient time to prepare for their visit to the park and to listen to the many birds around Kingfisher Cottage announcing the new day.

"See!" confirmed Olive to her parents. "I told you it would be better getting up around daylight for the birds' 'dawn chorus' as it gets light. They would have been in full song by six!" she added knowledgeably.

Toby and Libby stood there in the kitchen, loudly yawning, before Libby replied on behalf of the still-awakening parents. "Sorry, Olive. You're probably right but this is the best dawn chorus we can offer at this time of the morning! I thought I heard some distant thunder in the night but it seems to have cleared away. Seeing as it's so nice now why don't we all go for a quick walk and then come back for breakfast before heading to the park?" she suggested.

"Tell you what. You two go and I'll stay here and start preparing breakfast for when you get back," Toby offered.

"OK, sounds like a plan. Come on, Olive. Let's make tracks," requested Libby, ushering Olive outside Kingfisher Cottage.

Olive strolled ahead of her mum in the direction away from the manor entrance along the lane when she heard her mum shout. "No, Olive, let's go this way!" she insisted on signalling her back.

Olive turned around to see her mum standing by a cattle grid just up from the lodge and at the start of the sweeping driveway leading up to Didsvale Manor. She was looking at a notice that had been attached to the entrance gate adjacent to the cattle grid. It read, '**DANGER—KEEP OUT— SINKHOLES**'. "I think we'll go this way, Olive," she asserted.

As she caught up with her mum, Olive began to read the same sign and said, "But Mum. It says we're not allowed in. What if we fall into any of these holes?"

"Poppycock. I'm certain that wasn't here when we moved in. I'm intrigued. Come on, Olive! It would be nice to meet this mysterious Lord Didsvale with an early call of our own and introduce him to his new tenants. We won't be gobbled up by any sinkholes along the way. I promise. They say that an early bird catches the worm. Well let's see if Scumbali is the wriggly worm that Ahab warned us of!"

"But what about the things that Captain Ahab told us about him? Aren't you afraid?"

"What have we to be afraid of, Olive? Let's go and make our introductions to our landlord, the new Lord Didsvale. Come on let's get going! Someone's locked this side gate but we can always hop across the cattle grid. Don't worry, Olive. Take your time. You won't slip through it!" she assured.

The two gingerly crossed the cattle grid bars and made it to the other side without any mishaps. Then, with a certain amount of bravado, made their way up the sweeping drive towards the manor house until they reached the front of the building and stood by the austere front door. "What a splendid place, Olive. How would you like to live somewhere like this?" The end of Libby's question was drowned out by the deafening musical response to her pushing a large brass doorbell button. An Italian tenor's aria blasted out for several seconds before dying away.

Olive stood grimacing to her mum while covering her ears with her hands. They waited for a few seconds but there was no response. "Yes, it is a bit over the top isn't it, but let's give it one more go, eh?"

Without any say in the matter, Olive covered her ears once more as the doorbell was pressed for a second time. This time, Libby also covered her ears also in anticipation as another aria of similar ilk blasted down on them, before suggesting, "OK, no one bothering to answer the front door. Let's give the tradesman's entrance a go, Olive," only to find her bending down and peering through the large brass letterbox. "What do you think you're doing?" she asked her over-inquisitive daughter, anxiously.

"Shush, Mum. I can hear the faint laughter of voices echoing up the hallway from deep inside!"

"Never mind that. Let's try another way," Libby suggested.

They made their way round the side of the house to find what appeared to be the tradesman's entrance, where Libby tried again to get a response by knocking firmly on the finely crafted wooden panelled door. Again, to no avail. "There isn't much sign of life around here is there?" she observed.

Just as they were about to head back, Olive suddenly said, "Just a moment, Mum." Then, before Libby could do anything, Olive ran to the far corner of the manor and peered around the back.

"Like mother like daughter!" Libby whispered to herself as she quickly caught up with her adventurous daughter to see what was taking up her attention. They both saw two enormous white commercial trucks emblazed all over with the same company branding, **'Underpinning Inc.'**. "These will be the vehicles that Ahab told us about. Like he said, there isn't much sign of work around them and they are as clean as whistles. This signage looks pretty brand new to me. Look! Let's go and have a closer look," Libby suggested to Olive. "It won't do any harm."

They both scurried across the yard for a closer inspection. Olive went in one direction around to inspect one of the lorries, and her mum the other. Peering up and down each lorry, they met by the cab of the second one. "Did you find anything, Olive?" asked her mum.

"Nothing glaringly obvious on mine, except for a small piece of netting hanging down from the bottom of the rear tailgate," she reported back.

"Mmmm. Netting, eh? I'll ask your dad if it's of any significance to this supposed sinkhole work." Libby suddenly diverted her attention back to the lorry and noticed something odd. "Hang on, Olive. What's this?" One of the corners of a vinyl sticker on the driver's cab had flicked up. She then started to peel it back. "Look, Olive! There's another old sticker under here." Just as a capital letter **'D'** appeared on the paintwork underneath, Libby felt an arm on the back of her shoulder. "OK, Olive, that's a bit heavy handed," she complained. Then, as she turned around, the much larger figure of an adult male stood behind her. Olive had stood to one side with her eyes wide open with surprise.

"I'm sorry. I didn't mean to startle you both. Mya name's not Olive! Mya name is Lord Didsvale. Ora mora informally, Tarquini Scumbali," announced the eloquently dressed figure with a swarthy Mediterranean complexion, speaking in English but with a very odd Italian accent. "Can I help you both? Letta me guess. You must be the new tenants at Kingfisher Cottage!" he ascertained.

"Yes. That's us," replied Libby, sheepishly turning around to confront the surprise arrival, but she couldn't help but accidentally mimic the strange accent. "Mya nayma is..." and began again, "...sorry, my name is Libby Adamson and this is my daughter, Olive. I wanted to meet you personally, to introduce my family and to thank you on behalf of my husband for your generous offer on the rent for the cottage. My husband, Toby, is preparing breakfast for us all back at the cottage before we head off to the park. He apologises for not being able to come but says he looks forward to meeting you another day. We couldn't get an answer at the front or side of the manor so we wandered over here," she rambled, making it up as she went along.

"How very nice of you all!" he offered, insincerely, before suddenly changing the subject to ask searchingly, "Did you find anything interesting?" nodding towards the slightly peeled away sticker, noticing the same letter 'D' that Libby had revealed.

Libby quickly thought of an excuse to cover their snooping activity. "My husband's company is about to buy a new truck so I was just checking this one out for comparison. Very nice indeed," she answered, as convincingly as possible.

It seemed to work as he replied arrogantly in first person, "Tarquini Scumbali only buys the very best!" Then, finding his own way to cleverly masquerade the truth, he slowly pressed back down the sticker that revealed the letter 'D'. He claimed, "This particular truck was formerly used by another company in the village before I bought it." He then hesitated for a few seconds, during which time it was obvious to Libby and Olive that he was making it up as he went along. "It was called D...

76

D... D... **'Didsvale Landscaping'**," he stuttered out eventually, surprising himself with his sudden guile! As he finished smoothing the sticker back into position, his attention was caught by the keys and labels that Libby and Olive had each draped around their necks. Examining each label closely by hand while still around their necks, he asked menacingly, without waiting for a reply, "May I?" before bending forward and prying at each, then said, "Anda what do we have here?" Firstly, he read Olive's. "Mmmmm, 'Writing Desk'?" Then Libby's next. "Telescope?"

Without thinking, and in her state of excitement, Olive started to say, "Yes. And my dad has one for the 'En...'" She stopped herself just in time when she saw her mum's shaking head, indicating to her not to reveal the true answer. Fortunately, Tarquini hadn't noticed this.

"The Ennnnn...?" Tarquini prompted her to finish the word.

"The Ennnnntrance Key," Olive replied intelligently, as her mum gave her a 'thumbs-up' confirmation signal around waist height, once again out of Tarquini's eye line. She continued the false story without any further help. "That's right. It's the Entrance key to the park. Captain Ahab let Dad borrow it so we can get into the park later without bothering him," she explained.

"How trusting of dear old Captain McCrab!" said Tarquini, seemingly unconvinced by Olive's fragmented reply. As he stood back upright with his eyes closed deep in thought, Libby quickly pulled Olive towards her as they made a quick dart away from the truck and across the yard. She then shouted back to the over-inquisitive Lord Didsvale as they both disappeared around the corner of the building, "Sorry, Lord Didsvale. Must fly. Breakfast will be going cold. See you again soon I hope!"

"What a creepy guy," she whispered to Olive on exiting.

"He was a bit over the top wasn't he? A bit like that aftershave he was wearing!" chuckled Olive in reply.

Tarquini Scumbali snapped out of his deep trance. He spoke quietly under his breath to himself. "Yes. But you may see me sooner than you think, dear Adamsons. Damn! I must find out why they were snooping here and what those keys are for! I wonder if that young girl was going to say **'Engine Shed'** before she corrected herself? No one tricks the great Tarquini Scumbali, Lord of Didsvale, and gets away with it!" His voice had strangely changed into a south English accent. As he moved along the truck, he stroked the side panelling and appeared to address something hidden away on the inside, saying, "You did well on your first mission, my beauties! You will **all** have lots more work to do again soon!" A responsive hum came from inside the lorry and then died down. Then, with a more final manic laughter, Tarquini Scumbali made his way back across the courtyard and into Didsvale Manor.

# Chapter 8
## The Adamsons Return to Didsvale Park

The door of Kingfisher Cottage burst open, surprising Toby who was standing there with a full breakfast tray. "You're both cutting it fine. Breakfast is served," Toby announced.

Libby and Olive waited a few seconds to catch their breath after running all the way back down the drive from Didsvale Manor, before describing the encounter with Tarquini Scumbali to Toby over breakfast. Taken completely aback by their account he exclaimed, "Well! Well! It sounds as though Captain Ahab's description of Tarquini Scumbags was quite accurate after all. I take everything back. I wonder why he was so fascinated by your keys. I'm glad he thinks my key is for the entrance to the park and not to get into Peregrine's engine shed. I wonder why he was so inquisitive?" He quickly grabbed his tablet. "What was the name of that company you saw on the lorry?" he asked Libby.

"'**Underpinning Inc.**'," she replied.

"And the other one Scumbali mentioned?" he added.

"It was called."

She hesitated for a second and then Olive jumped in. "**Didsvale Landscaping!**" answered the eager youngster.

"Well remembered, Olive!" Libby complimented.

"Yes, Dad. Definitely! '**Didsvale Landscaping**'!"

"Why?" they both asked.

"Why?" Toby replied, putting down his tablet. "Because, according to my search, those two companies don't exist, and there isn't an official company application pending for '**Underpinning Inc.**'. It looks as though our revered Lord Didsvale has something to hide!"

"How strange," Libby mused and then, turning to Olive, repeated some of Toby's words, "... somathinga toa hyda!" Olive laughed out somewhat nervously at her mum's attempt to mimic Tarquini's unconvincing accent.

Toby looked bemused at the in-joke and made no comment. Indeed, he took on a look of concern. "How strange indeed! But we haven't got time to ponder. Let's discuss later," he suggested. "It's seven already. We've only got thirty minutes to get to the park and meet the captain. Come on, we need to get our skates on!"

"Oh, and don't forget this, Olive!" Libby ran back and picked up an object from the living room table and gripped it in her cupped outstretched hand before presenting it forwards to Olive.

"Wow, thanks, Mum. Nearly forgot it by rushing," she answered with relief as she held the treasured item aloft. It was a compass contained in a silver case that had belonged to her late grandfather. On the reverse read the engraving '*Never Lose your Direction in Life—GramPs x*'.

"OK everyone. Let's rush. Have we all got our key?" Libby shouted impatiently, holding her own key firmly on show to the others.

"Yes! Of course," they replied in unison, displaying each of their keys simultaneously.

"Off we go then, fast as we can. Onwards and upwards! I think I may have just heard some thunder in the distance. There may be some rain coming to clear up this stifling summer heat." Libby was still speaking these words as she opened the front door, only to be startled by an unexpected female visitor who almost fell in to the cottage with surprise at the door opening suddenly. She began to apologise with a very hoity-toity plummy accent.

"Oh. I'm terribly sorry. I presume you are the new arrivals to Kingfisher Cottage? I'm sorry to disturb you all so early. Please allow me to introduce myself. I'm Dotty D'eath. That's pronounced **De...Ath** by the way," she corrected assertively. "Anyway, when I heard you were moving in, I felt that I must call round and offer you this little gift from the villagers."

"Oh. How lovely and kind," replied Libby as she grasped the potted plant in a decorative vase being offered to her, before placing it carefully on the window ledge just inside the cottage doorway. At this point, Toby had taken obvious notice of the attractive features of the tall, slim visitor who stood there dressed in a long floral dress. Her long black hair topped with a quirky purple beret, had him staring transfixed, intoxicated by her expensive perfume until Libby gave him a quick dig in the ribs, snapping him back to reality. "And this is my 'loving husband', Toby, and my daughter, Olive." Peering from either side of Libby, Toby and Olive extended a single hand each, which Dotty shook vigorously together with a large warm smile. "You must excuse us but we are in a bit of a hurry. I'm sure we'll see each other around though," Libby said apologetically as the group headed through the door. These were her parting words as the door-catch of Kingfisher Cottage firmly closed and locked behind them.

"Oh, we'll definitely be seeing each other around!" Dotty replied oddly under her breath, as the Adamsons made their way down the drive.

Passing her open-top sports car parked nearby, Toby commented, "Wow, she's got some style."

"Yes, and she can keep it!" replied Libby to her errant husband with a hint of jealousy displayed by a quick prod in his back as they rushed to their appointment with Ahab. "I bet her middle name is Rosalind. They'd be quite fitting initials wouldn't they, D.R. Dee ATH... or Doctor Death more like it!" she quipped.

Olive laughed out loud saying, "Mum. That's really funny and naughty!" before adding and continuing to laugh helplessly towards her father, "Dad! I think you're in trouble and I'm with you, Mum. I think she stinks!"

Libby took on a thoughtful expression before suddenly exclaiming, "That's it, Olive! She does stink! And Scumbali strangely stinks just the same way!"

"What do you mean, Mum?"

"Oh, nothing. It's just a hunch," Libby replied dismissively, before breaking into a jog in order to make up for lost time.

Toby was keeping pace, overhearing the conversation. "What's that bit about a hunch?" he asked out of Olive's earshot.

"It was more than a hunch," Libby replied quietly. "I knew I'd smelt that perfume she was wearing before. It was the same concoction that Scumbali had around his mush mixed in with his cheap aftershave. And that hunch also tells me that the distant thunder I thought I heard a few hours ago, wasn't thunder after all. I'll tell you what that really was!" Before Toby had the chance to respond, Libby chipped back in. "It was the sound of Dotty Droopy-drawers driving back across the cattle grid from Didsvale Manor after her tryst with Lord Scumbags! They're up to something. Quick, we need to keep ahead of the game." At which point, the Adamsons changed from a gentle jog into a brisk running pace to be punctual for their meet up with Ahab.

As they disappeared out of view, Dotty D'eath opened her designer handbag and pulled out her cell phone to make a call, which was then answered promptly. "Hello, Dotty Dear heart. Have you successfully made your introduction to our new found friends?"

"Absolutely, Tarky Warky!" she replied with a familiar seductive tone.

"Wonderful. Is the listening device in place?" enquired Tarquini Scumbali.

"Yes. It's hidden in my gift inside the cottage!" Dotty quipped, with an arrogant sounding laugh.

"Excellent. Good work. And the Adamsons?" he further enquired.

"They're on their way back to the park," Dotty confirmed.

"If they come back for any reason, we can pick up everything they say in the cottage. That is if they do come back **or** go straight to jail, which is even more likely! However, we may have to move faster than I thought, Dotty darling," confirmed the manic tones of Tarquini Scumbali. "Let's stick to plan 'A' for now. Convene your meeting to go ahead as agreed this evening. We'll take things from there," he instructed. "You were brilliant in hoodwinking those numpty councillor colleagues of yours into approving our superb 'sinkhole' story to close the reserve. They really did fall hook, line and 'sinker' for that one with that fictitious forged surveyor's report of yours. Get it! Dotty, sinker! Hee! Hee! Hee! You know what to do, poppet. Just make sure it all goes ahead smoothly. As Chief Planning Officer for the parish council you must tread as carefully as those dainty toes of yours have ever trodden before!" He added flatteringly.

"Oh Tarky Warky, you're such a rascally punster. Don't worry. Leave that in my capable hands. It'll go as smooth as my ultra-smooth silk stockings. Bye, bye, Tarky. Mmmwaaa!" she drooled seductively as they ended their call.

"Bye, bye, Dotty Wotty! Mmmwaa! To you too, a thousand times back." Tarquini Scumbali then suddenly changed his tone as he heard the click come from Dotty's phone ending their conversation, and diverted his attention to the bank of dozens of TV monitors stacked inside his office. He was speaking directly at one monitor, where he could see the lorry parked with its sinister contents outside. "But first, we must take care of our goody-woody Adamson family. Won't we, my lovelies!" he said to his drones as they nestled inside the lorries in readiness of his devious instructions. He tested the listening device hidden within the vase placed on the window ledge just inside Kingfisher Cottage. Clearly audible from outside the window of the cottage, he could pick up the distinctive caw of a lone jackdaw. "Loud and clear. Loud and clear!" he whispered to himself with satisfaction. "Yes! That is if those nosy Adamsons have any chance to come back!" He ended with another spate of his trademark manic laughter.

# Chapter 9
## *The Same Evening at Didsvale Parish Hall*

At Didsvale Village Hall, the council clerk was about to make an important announcement to the local councillors. The locals used this tiny multi-functional hall on many occasions, week-to-week. However, on this particular evening, all the usual mundane items on the agenda were cancelled due to the importance of an extraordinary meeting convened by Dotty D'eath. Secretary to the Council, Cecil Stumpwart, addressed the formal gathering. "Dear councillors. Thank you all for your one hundred per cent attendance at this meeting. This extraordinary meeting has been arranged by our revered colleague here because of its unique importance to our village and its future prosperity." He nodded to Dotty, who reciprocated back at the compliment, before formally announcing to the full room of the committee members. "So, the only item on our agenda to discuss this evening is namely... 'Planning permission requested by Tarquini Scumbali, Lord Didsvale of Didsvale Manor, to build an eco-friendly power generating facility on Didsvale Manor estate on the site of the old nature reserve."

Dotty D'eath raised herself out of her seat in anticipation of the council secretary's last words before addressing the group sat in a row immediately in front of her, and began to speak with her usual self-importance. "Thank you, my honourable colleague," Dotty boomed as Cecil lowered himself sheepishly to his seat at the authoritative interruption. "As Chief Planning Officer of this council I would like to make this statement. Hopefully, it will save us all a great deal of time and we can get on with the rest of our relaxing evenings." She looked at each of the other six members of the gathered committee with an air of confidence combined with unchallenged arrogance. "As far as I'm concerned, this matter is a foregone conclusion! Lord Scumbali has wanted nothing but to support this village ever since the day he bought Didsvale Manor from our dear departed friend and previous owner, Professor Peregrine Greylag. Tarquini Scumbali has brought his much-respected Italian aristocracy to our quaint, humble village and embellished every single green corner of it by virtue of his concern for the welfare of every single one of us. Lord Scumbali bought Didsvale Manor from Professor Greylag in the belief that he could save it from dereliction by underpinning it at his own expense, and filling in the treacherous sinkholes caused by the ancient mine workings, which I showed professional evidence of to you all at our last meeting. We mourn Professor Greylag's passing and appreciate what he did for our village, but now is the time to put our sympathies to one side and put things into a more realistic perspective. Had he still been with us, then I'm absolutely certain he would have given this project his full blessing to see Didsvale Manor saved in such a way. Would you not all agree with these sentiments?" she asked the fully attentive councillors, who all nodded vigorously in agreement. Dotty D'eath continued. "Lord Scumbali, as he likes to be known, has dug very deep into his pocket to make safe all those life threatening sinkholes, and I personally saw him weeping with sorrow at the prospect of having to close our beloved nature reserve and the miniature train rides that all our families have enjoyed throughout the years. However, from the disappointment of losing our nature park and miniature railway, I am able to propose a new, lucrative endeavour thought up by the brilliant vision of Lord Scumbali, which will benefit our wonderful community for future generations to come. I'm confident that it will bring great prosperity to the village of Didsvale." At this point, she brought out a paper document from her briefcase, then unfolded it before offering it to the nearest councillor and gestured for her to hand it around the group. Dotty D'eath then announced in the most melodramatic way, "Elected members of Didsvale Village Parish Council, I give you…" she took a deep breath before the next melodramatic addition to her speech… "The master plan for Didsvale's world-beating, largest land wind turbine generator." A nearby member raised a questioning hand but she was given an immediate gesture by Dotty to put it down again, which she did without protest. "This will not only be a world beating eco-friendly project, but we are promised by the mercurial Lord Scumbali that it will generate enough power to provide free power to the villagers of Didsvale for as long as the wind blows across our fair land. As Lord Scumbali's 'pièce de résistance', he has also generously offered to pay for the long-awaited repairs to the roof of this civic building— AND—to financially support all the local groups using the hall, which most of us are members of! How fortunate we are to have such a wonderful benefactor as Lord Tarquini Scumbali!" Dotty D'eath finished her speech with such a sensational flurry. "So! Members of the planning committee, I move that this submission be approved unanimously and without delay!" Dotty then sat down to await the council's decision.

"All those in favour?" asked Cecil, now stood up on his feet again. The councillors looked along the row at each other with various forms of approving expressions and nods. Six approving hands then shot up in response before Dotty raised her own hand victoriously into the air. "Moved and approved unanimously," acclaimed Cecil to rapturous applause from every committee member. "This is the dawn of a new chapter in the history of Didsvale. I must insist on your complete confidentiality in this matter, as I shall be announcing it to the villagers at tonight's event, where I look forward to us all being in attendance. Shan't we?" She looked around at the suppressed, obeying nods of the agreeing committee. "This committee will be the envy of every village for miles around," Dotty proclaimed, before hurrying out of the village hall with a beaming smile. She returned to her car parked around the corner and then made a further mobile call to Tarquini Scumbali. "Mission accomplished, Tarky Warky!" she gushed.

"Excellent!" Tarquini responded with glee. "I knew you wouldn't fail me, my Scrumptious Pie. It's onward and upwards from now on. Upwards into the sky with our magnificent mammoth wind turbine on that unsightly nature reserve!" he added. "We've just a couple of loose ends to tie up. That weirdo, Captain Ahab, is nicely set up with a snap of him leaving on his boat for some stupid magic potion with my planted stolen antique carriage clock. I've reported that fictitious robbery of the manor to the local police, who will have him in handcuffs as soon as he returns from his fantasy island. That just leaves the second loose end of the snooping Adamsons. I can't take any risks because they possibly know more than we think. I found two of them snooping around the manor grounds earlier. I think I should pay them a visit at the engine shed later. I'll use their Captain friend's freedom to trade with in return for their utmost confidentiality and loyalty. Once I've finished with them, they'll be shamefully run out of the village, never to return," he added enthusiastically before ending. "So, my Sweet Sugar Sorbet, it's imperative that we continue to keep our lovely liaison private and not to blow our cover. We can then plan ahead blissfully together. Or shall I say, plan ahead blissfully together with the future Lady Didsvale!" he added teasingly.

"Oh Tarky! You are such a tantalising genius! Yes! I also got a suspicious negative vibe from our new arrivals when I called in to say hello after our last little…" she paused. "…tete a tete!" she added with a childish giggle.

"I'll see you at the village hall this evening, Pumpkin." Tarquini finished their conversation before looking into the mirror nearby on the wall and saying with excessive self-adulation, "Yes, Tarky Warky. What a tantalising genius you are!" He then broke out into his normal manic laughter before composing himself once again. "OK my lovely droney wonies! Let's finish netting the trees and keep those damn birds from holding up any progress. There's just the one left to do, and then we've covered all of that blasted forest and it's finally goodbye to that hindering nature reserve and those pesky birds." At which moment, his hands began to tap into the keyboard placed in front of the bank of video screens. He could see his computer commands enable the roofs of the two large trucks parked outside, to slowly open upwards. A large black drone appeared from one of them, lifting itself vertically from its housing to be followed by six other smaller versions. The larger drone glided silently across to the other truck and descended inside it. Almost like worker bees responding to their queen, the smaller drones grouped themselves in formation, hovering at an equal distance above the other truck, waiting for their orders. The mother drone appeared, dragging up a massive piece of folded green netting. Very carefully and deliberately, it hooked a part of the netting onto a corner of each of the smaller drones until they all shared the entire piece between them. From his operation nerve centre, Tarquini expertly guided them outwards until the entire netting was held taught and completely flat. With a further few taps into his keyboard, he commanded the six drones to make a flight path towards the last section of trees on the nature reserve. After a few seconds, they arrived directly over the designated point and lowered the netting precisely into position to cover the last few hundred square metres of open tree canopy left on the reserve. With self-congratulation, Tarquini muttered as he witnessed the successful operation. "Careful as you go, my babies. That's it. Mission completed! Game, Set and Match! No net faults!" He quipped, clapping his hands rapidly with satisfaction. The mother drone and support crafts were then guided back into their truck to await Tarquini's next instructions. "OK Adamsons. We have a little unfinished business!" Tarquini whispered menacingly to himself as he draped his coat around his shoulders, making his way out of sinister environment, striding determinedly towards the engine shed.

# Chapter 10
# Ahab Departs for Pamona Atoll

As promised, the three newly appointed temporary park keepers arrived breathlessly outside the Didsvale Park entrance just before seven thirty a.m. Looking around, Libby mused to the other two. "You never guess what?"

Toby and Olive looked at each other before Toby answered coyly. "What?"

"From rushing, we've only forgotten to bring the rucksack with the phones, computer tablet, chargers, my drawing pad, binoculars and food."

"It's too late to go back and it's almost time to go into the park!" stated Toby. "I'm sure we can live without those things for a day. We are on holiday and having a break from work, don't forget. It might do us good being without them for a change!"

"True," Libby agreed.

Olive spared no more time and rushed towards the door, then began knocking and reciting the captain's words. "'*Knock on the side door seven times, then pause seven seconds for number eight.*'" The old railway semaphore signal arm inside the park gate, magically lifted upwards to release the gate catch from the inside. "There you go!" she said in response, "And I didn't forget and we weren't late!" she added victoriously.

They all shuffled quickly through the park entrance as the door started to close and subsequently lock behind them. They wasted no further time by scurrying directly to Bosun's Cabin. When they arrived, there was no apparent sign of the captain outside. However, just as Libby went to knock on the door, she was startled by Ahab's sudden appearance as he opened the door exactly at the same time. The captain stood there dressed in his usual nautical attire along with a large traditional navy blue sailor's kit bag with chord strappings. Without time for small talk or any of the storytelling he entertained them with the day before, he began to speak hurriedly. "Professor Peregrine's trusty old exploration boat, the Pretty pol, is as spick and span as she ever was and ready to sail once again. Quick, we have no time to lose. Right, where's my Ship's Bell Officer?" he asked, looking directly at Olive for a helpful response.

"Here Captain!" Olive replied efficiently with a salute.

"OK all. Give me a few minutes to get down to the old ferry landing before you strike the bell. Olive! You remember how it goes don't you?" he added as he sped away.

"Affirmative Captain!" Olive gave the departing Captain a second salute as she whispered his second rhyme to herself. *"'As the last of eight bells ends its ring, mighty Argyll will take to wing. He'll billow your sails and give you speed, to Pamona Atoll for the juice we need.'* But how will Argyll know where you are, and how will you get back?" Olive shouted loudly to the departing figure.

"Oh, I nearly forgot," he replied. "My apologies! It goes... *'Ring eight bells again while you quack like a duck and Argyll will return without any luck!'* Argyll was well programmed by Peregrine in advance, so don't worry. He'll find me all right for a return ticket there and back. Remember! You must trust the professor all the time!" reassured the captain as his voice faded into the distant woods, as he made his way to the ferry landing along the river path towards the far end of the park.

A short while passed by. "I think that's more than a few minutes. Time to ring the bell," Olive cried out impatiently.

"OK. Go for it," Libby urged.

Olive reached for the piece of rope attached to the bell's clanger and began swinging it from side to side. As the bell started to clang, she shouted loudly, "*As the last of eight bells ends its ring, mighty Argyll will take to wing. He'll billow your sails and give you speed, to Pamona Atoll for the juice we need*'." As the eighth bell struck, Olive turned around, revealing the largest beaming smile she could fit on her tiny face, proudly claiming, "Mission accomplished, Captain Ahab!" as if he was still there.

The sound of the bell still echoed deep into the forest, gradually getting fainter and fainter a good few seconds after she finished the last clang. The three all stood in silent anticipation in the now complete stillness under the trees by Bosun's Cabin. A single leaf fell at their feet in response to the tiniest of breezes. A tiny breeze that got stronger and stronger until the three figures were holding onto each other, fighting against what had now become a mini hurricane. The gaps of blue morning sky piercing through the tree canopy above, were suddenly blackened out as a huge figure swooped overhead. "It's Argyll! It's Argyll!" screamed Olive to the others above the noisy downdraught of the gigantic bird's swooping wings.

The windy disturbance subsided as quickly as it came as

Toby, who was still looking up in astonishment, spoke to himself in resigned contrition. "Yes. So that must be the fabled Argyll! My apologies to you, Ahab! It seems you're not a rung short of a rope ladder after all!" He humbly sighed for not taking the captain seriously enough.

Down at the Didsvale Ferry landing, Ahab slowly regained his breath after his hurried departure. He was standing upright, clinging onto the mast of the tiny sailboat grasping a rope, which he used to keep his boat secure alongside the ferry landing. His rucksack was slung firmly over his shoulder awaiting Argyll's arrival. Ahab felt in his pocket and lifted out Peregrine's small glass phial bottle. He tapped it with an air of confidence before slipping it securely to where it came from. As the little boat started to rock gently from side to side, he felt something hitting his foot. He reached down and lifted up the offending object. With a look of intrigue, he was examining an exquisite carriage clock. Despite his limited knowledge on antiques, he could instantly see that it was something of value. He looked puzzled as to how it came to be there, shrugged his shoulders and placed the heavy object safely inside his rucksack before tightly tying it up again. As he did so, Tarquini's mother drone finished recording every clear telescopic detail of Ahab's 'find' from high above on the other side of the river before gliding away undetected in the direction of Didsvale Manor. The morning's blue sky darkened just as the boat's large single sail began to flutter. Soon, it was billowing fully as Argyll's unmistakable gigantic outline appeared overhead.

Captain Ahab shouted as loud as he could above the commotion. "Ah! So you're the mighty Argyll! I never doubted you, Peregrine! Not for one minute! Off to Pamona

Atoll we go, Argyll! I believe you know the way! Anchor's Away!" At which point, he let go of the rope to allow the downdraft of Argyll's massive wings to blow himself and the tiny 'Pretty Pol' away from the ferry landing, down the River Babble, and towards the open estuary and out into the open sea towards Pamona Atoll.

The Adamsons had rushed down to the ferry landing as fast as they could just as everything was calming down, and the blue sky was reappearing. The isolated figure of Olive stood at the end of the ferry landing peering out to sea with sharp eyes. In the distance, she could just about make out a small boat with the captain clinging horizontally onto the mast and two Squibrels peering from the top of his rucksack. With the powerful wings of Argyll flapping effortlessly behind, they gradually disappeared over the horizon and onwards to Pamona Atoll. "Safe journey, Captain Ahab, Stanley and Livingstone," said Olive, while smiling fondly. "We'll keep believing in Professor Peregrine for you," she ended, waving her hand that was also tightly holding the writing desk key that Ahab had entrusted her with.

# Chapter 11
## The Engine Shed

Toby broke the eerie silence in an attempt to bring the trio back to reality with a practical comment. "Looks like we're all in charge, then. Come on! No time to waste! Let's all see what lies in store at the engine shed." The group headed off back down the path towards the nearby engine shed. They soon noticed the railway track peeking through the bramble to the side, and eventually stopped when they saw the circular shaped building that Ahab had described to them.

"Well, here we are," Libby announced to the others. "It's bigger than I thought to house miniature steam trains. I'd say it's an even larger area than Kingfisher Cottage and its gardens," she calculated.

Well, it was intended for Peregrine's original larger collection," replied Toby, while scrutinising the building in detail. He was eyeing a structure about twenty metres in diameter with a brick circular outer wall approximately three metres high. It had a wooden dome-shaped roof built on top, doubling the overall height at its apex at the centre. At this meeting point, a square tin air vent was fitted into the roof for releasing the train engine smoke and steam from inside the shed. The entrance to the building appeared to be through a large padlocked wooden double door at the front where a single narrow railway track also entered. "I don't know how

Professor Peregrine ever expected to get a steam train running out of here again. He would have needed thousands of litres of water and tonnes of coal to power them with, but not with those. Look!" at which point he signalled with a nod of his head to the others for them to look in the same direction and share what he was looking at. Mostly hidden behind large bracken and ferns, was a severely rusted water tower with its water pipe now split and completely opened up. Just to one side of it, but less disguised, could be seen an open wooden coal storage compartment, now laid completely bare except for a thin layer of tiny coal fragments coving the rotting floor. Alongside the building were four partly dismantled wooden passenger carriages stationed on a small section of extended track.

Toby was stroking the sides of his face with one hand as if in deep thought, and then turned slowly to the others. "Tell you what! Before we go in, and while we're close to the river bridge, I'd like to have a little informal inspection of Tarquini Scumbali's 'sinkhole exclusion zone'," as he described to them with an air of suspicion. "You two wait here. Don't enter the engine shed until I return. I'll be as quick as I can."

"Just don't snoop too much, Toby, you've not met him yet. He seems a bit creepy and suspicious to me. I wouldn't get on the wrong side of him if I were you," she pleaded.

"Don't worry. I'll be careful. I'm not looking for a formal introduction. I'm looking for something more 'informal' let's say!" he explained before rushing from the engine shed.

"Yes. Be careful, Dad. Don't go near any sink holes," Olive added, still innocently taken in by the frightening nature of Tarquini Scumbali's warning signs.

Toby rushed at pace along the course of the old railway

track until arriving at the bridge, where it crossed over the River Babble, then into the old reserve with the old River Babble Station sign still intact. He stopped to read two separate signs standing nearby, which had been partly damaged by evidence of a large footprint across it and murmured quietly to himself, "'Danger, Keep Out, Sinkholes'. Sinkholes my eye! He then read the other sign. "'Dangerous Rotting Bridge—May Collapse'. Well, it looks sturdy enough to me! What are you *really* up to Scumbags? I think that you're the only rotter around here," he asked himself further of the new Lord Didsvale. As he turned forwards again he noticed a glint of reflected light coming from inside a large wooden bat box attached to a nearby tree halfway up. Thinking nothing more of it, Toby ignored the sign and made his way over the bridge and onto the reserve, then parted with the railway track to take an unmarked route deep into the reserve thicket. After what seemed endless yards of fighting with the undergrowth, he came to a wide-open area closely surrounded by large trees. As he pulled the remaining branches hindering his progress, he saw the edge of the front bucket of an earth-digging machine. It was painted in green patterned camouflage and was seemingly deliberately parked well-hidden out of view. Without hesitating any further, he entered the sparse open area, which had been deliberately covered in loose grass. He stopped and looked down at what his foot had just nudged against. He reached down into the undergrowth and untangled the end of a wooden post. He wrenched it out to eye level, where the full extent of a previously abandoned signpost had been left. The flat board on top of the post read 'Nature Reserve Lake Station'. Toby screwed his face up in deep thought. As he went to throw the sign back into the undergrowth, he saw some netting poking out from underneath the loose grass. He leant forward to investigate, but found his footing starting to give way on some soft soil and lost balance. Before he could step back to safety, found himself sliding down a steep, soil embankment. As he fell several more feet, some old dead tree roots abruptly stopped his descent. From his perilous position he peered downwards. The sunlight above was piercing through the grass above him, which had been deliberately scattered over a large extent of green netting. Toby now found himself suspended perilously in a huge, cavernous, bowl-shaped area with flat flooring underground. The whole area must have been one hundred metres deep.

The outer wall had been made secure with a cladding of large stones held into position inside a wire framework, except for the point where Toby had fallen in, which looked due for imminent completion. On the far opposite side of the cavern, he could easily make out a flight of metal stairs descending from ground level. A gentle humming then suddenly broke Toby's concentration which reverberated around the whole underground chasm, increasing in volume into an amplified, deafening noise. He wanted to cover up both ears as he clung onto the tree roots with all his strength. Then, despite the disturbance, he managed to swing himself upwards to claw his way back up onto the embankment with the help of a few more protruding roots acting as his steps. He reappeared back safely from underneath the loose grass and netting that had led to his sudden and temporary disappearance. However, his safety now seemed in doubt as a more subdued humming seemed to come from directly overhead. Shielding his eyes from the piercing rays of sunlight with one hand he gazed up to see the light slowly disappearing through the group of trees next to him. He could just about make out the shape of large netting being draped onto them from something hovering above, before some of its outer edges dangled high above his head. A few startled birds, disturbed by the commotion, had started to fly away in fright from their nests as their homes were being completely enveloped. Without looking up or turning around for even one more second, Toby raced back the same way he entered the reserve by retracing the flattened grass track he'd left on the way in. Before too long, he scampered back across the River Babble bridge and stood breathless for a few minutes, leaning on one of Tarquini's warning signs. The deafening humming noises had long since gone and were now replaced by the soft comforting gentle swishing sound of the reeds on the river bank in the afternoon breeze. Toby took in a deep breath. "Well. That was informal!" he sighed as he reflected on his earlier comment. He darted back to the engine shed as fast as he could. It wasn't long before he re-joined the others outside the shed doors.

"Everything OK, Toby? We were getting a little concerned where you were," asked Libby concernedly.

"Oh yes! Well, no, not really." Toby quickly changed his mind and confessed, after trying to play down the significance of what he'd discovered. "I wasn't expecting to drop in on Tarquini Scumbali today, but I did seem to drop into something else quite extraordinary! It looks like the devious devil is up to something. Why would he go to the trouble of draining the old lake and throwing protective netting over the trees?"

"Drained the lake and netted the trees?" Libby repeated, astounded by Toby's revelation. "Why on earth would he do such a thing to such a beautiful place? And I'm pretty sure it could be an illegal thing to do! Those poor birds! Well, we'll see about that!" she added angrily.

Toby didn't want to alarm the others with a more detailed account of his earlier dangerous encounter inside the covered cavern, so decided to play it down a little before explaining. "I've absolutely no idea. Yes, as I explained, the old lake seems to have been completely drained and excavated, then camouflaged with loose grass and netting over the top."

"Wait a minute. You definitely saw netting, didn't you?" Libby asked for clarification before looking at Olive.

"Yes. Why do you ask?" Toby queried.

Olive had taken in every word of the conversation before responding to her mother's prompting look. "Not green netting by any chance, Dad?"

"Yes, it was. But how did you know that?" he asked with bemusement.

"Because that was the colour of the netting hanging down from one of Tarquini's trucks I saw before he crept up and surprised us at the manor," she explained.

"Was it really, Olive? Well remembered! You're turning into a real super-sleuth," Libby said proudly to her daughter, who stood there proudly blushing.

"As you suggested, Libby. Scumball is definitely up to something," Toby stated, before switching his attention back to the large front door of the engine shed. "OK. Let's see where we get to with our keys shall we?" He led the others towards the large locked wooden doors before stopping to inspect the outside of the building and concluded, "The only way in appears to be through these doors. No windows either, strange to say!" He pulled the key around his neck and slotted it into a rusty padlock hanging from the door. With a few wiggles of the key, it clicked and without any further effort, the door started to creak open inwardly almost on its own. Libby and Olive followed Toby into the engine shed, being careful not to trip on the piece of old railway track underfoot. Toby hung the key back around his neck.

The three stood holding hands just inside the gloomy building, blinking as their eyes adjusted to the difference of the semi-light from the bright sunlight they had left outside. Their eyes were simultaneously attracted to shafts of light, shooting through the tin air vent in the centre of the building's domed roof and downwards into the shed. The shafts came to an abrupt halt against a large shape that stood facing towards them on the other side of the turntable. One shaft of light fell directly onto a black metal plaque on the top front of the object, sharply illuminating some shiny brass lettering spelling out the words, 'Flying Cootsman'. Toby broke the eerie silence with excitement. "Look! There she is! Peregrine's immaculate 'Flying Cootsman'." He felt the end of a piece of dangling chord brush against his face, which he immediately recognised as a light switch and gave it a quick tug. As a result, a line of long strip lights running all around the top of the retaining wall, together with some similar smaller lights surrounding the edge of the air vent above, slowly began to flicker and pop into action until they were all fully on and illuminating the whole building. They all hid their eyes from the new artificial brightness and blinked for a few seconds as they became accustomed to it.

"Wow. What a fantastic piece of machinery. You can see just how much of his dedicated time, care and attention Peregrine gave up to re-building her! She looks magnificent!" Toby cried out. He stood there, mesmerised by the magnificent piece of engineering facing him with her boiler, cab and coal tender painted immaculately in apple green; with black wheels and silver steel pistons; a black boiler front, two extending wind deflectors and chimney with her name just underneath it; two bright silver buffers adorning the front, affixed to a bright red metal plate. Last, but not least, the name 'Flying Cootsman' sat resplendent in a semi-circular cast-iron plaque, which was repeated on both sides of the engine's boiler. Toby continued with his expert detailed description. "She's pretty much unblemished and a great compliment to the full-size famous mainline steam engine of its day. That is except for those rotting leaves around the fixed tender which seemed to have blown down from the end of that length of old water pipe hose attached to that air vent up there," he pointed out. "It's as if Peregrine had only just cleaned her and was half expecting her to steam out of the shed again. It was that forlorn hope that probably kept him going. It's almost as though he was still determined to have her steaming around the park again, one day. Maybe? Who knows?" he said turning to Libby, who gave a sympathetic smile back.

"Who knows?" she responded.

"Or, Dad?" Olive jumped in enthusiastically. "Maybe you'll be able to give her a second run out when you work out how to operate her?" She added encouragingly, "Even if it's just through those shed doors and back again!" Mouth still agape since the lighting came fully on, Olive looked all around the roundhouse shed in front of her before commenting imaginatively to her father, "Blimey Dad! I bet this is what the inside of a flying saucer looks like!"

"If there was such a thing!" he responded pragmatically.

"You bet there is!" responded Olive unflinchingly.

"Now that's enough, you two. Let's leave that argument

for another day," ordered Libby, bringing the conversation to an end with a subtle laugh. "Toby! Let's go play more seek and find!" she asserted, indicating for the three to proceed further forward into the shed. "As it says on my key label, 'seek and ye shall find'! Those words are turning out to be more key to the conversation aren't they!" she quipped.

"Eh. I thought it was my job to be the family punster!" Toby responded with a quick burst of laughter.

After becoming even more accustomed to the improved lighting conditions, they could now make out every single detail of the small building's structure. The same section of railway track that came into the building where they had all entered, eventually extended onto a central turntable. Spiralling outwards, spaced out evenly around the outside of the central turntable and almost touching the outer wall were seven more lengthy pieces of track with stopper buffers positioned at either end. They moved a few feet closer to the edge of the turntable to examine it in more detail. As they stepped over each piece of track Olive began to point at individual plaques fixed to each of the buffers. Some displayed names. "Oh look. How sad. These must be where Peregrine's trains were kept before he had to sell them off. I presume the other spurs were for possible new trains for when the railway re-started. I wouldn't be surprised if Peregrine had that ambition. What a shame it didn't come to fruition." Just about legible through their dusty condition were the position numbers and names of the professor's three original trains. **TWO—BULLFINCH, THREE—NUTHATCH, FOUR—SPARROW HAWK.** They inspected further. There appeared to be a circular gear wheel running around the inside of the turntable to make it revolve around and line up with any other selected track.

Toby picked up on this. "How sad that all of the other stabling 'spurs' are now empty? That's the name given to these tracks on the outside of the turntable. Spurs!" he confirmed. "They were all going to be full exactly as you guessed, Olive. How sad!" He then went further around the outside, with the others following him. They finally stood next to Flying Cootsman. "What a fantastic specimen of an engine," Toby glowed enthusiastically. He strode to the end of the engine to look around the rear of it. "Here's her engine number and name on the buffer in pride of place, first and foremost. His pride and joy! **ONE—FLYING COOTSMAN**," he pronounced formally to the others. "What a pity she never had the chance to fire up and steam beyond those doors again!" he added nostalgically while nodding in the direction of the shed's entrance.

"Isn't it fascinating, Olive? Olive?" Libby's question went unanswered as she turned around to find that she hadn't followed them. "Olive? Where are you," she called out again.

Just as she did, Olive's voice echoed from underneath the turntable, "Under here!"

"Where?" Libby called out.

"Here. Underneath the turntable," Olive directed.

Toby and Libby rushed over to the far end of the turntable, where they saw a small open hatch and several ladder rungs leading downwards. They descended down several feet, closing the hatch behind them, to find Olive standing at the bottom next to a light switch cord that she had pulled to illuminate the area. "What do you think of this then?" she asked the others as they joined her, standing open-mouthed at what greeted them. They were all now standing on a circular platform suspended directly underneath the turntable. Looking at the curved wall around them, they noticed nearly every square metre of its wooden-clad surface had been covered with coloured, neatly drawn sketches of various birds. Pinned to the wall, every so often, were chalkboards written on with strange letters and numbers.

Libby began to examine the sketches in more detail. "These all look like local species. It appears Peregrine kept a personal record of them, assuming these are all his sketches. Quite an artist was our professor! A man of many talents," she concluded. "Those strange equations on the chalkboards must be the formulas he worked on for his SMEW invention that Ahab told us about."

"Blimey. So this is where Professor Greylag worked," deduced Toby.

Libby focussed her attention to what looked like Peregrine's living area. "He must have actually lived down here as well at times," she added, while making a gesturing with a nod with her head at a small bed, wardrobe and desk, with a small sink and a mirror fixed next to them. She walked over to a gap along the wall where a metal side rail had been placed. She leant over it, peering into a deep chasm covered in thick tree roots, which snaked around and around, descending deeper and deeper before disappearing from the half-light into the complete black abyss beneath.

"Wow! Amazing! I don't believe it, said Toby joining her. "This must be what Ahab was on about, the ancient fabled tree. Not a fable after all! These must be its old dead roots. Anyway, I'm not climbing down there, that's for sure," he reassured. "I can see how it gave him a good foundation to build his engine shed on though. What a genius!"

"What's that over there?" Olive suddenly quizzed. Across from where they stood, she picked out an old sheet left covering a large object underneath. She raced over to inspect and took a brief peek underneath it by lifting one edge of the sheet. Toby and Libby looked on as Olive slowly raised the blanket, tantalisingly slowly, to reveal the protected item hidden underneath. Then, like a master chef revealing a special dish, announced very formally, "Et voila! One writing desk!" She gave her new possession a loving, reassuring rub and pulled up a nearby chair before continuing, "And one key to fit it I hope?" Unable to hold back her excitement any longer, she pulled Peregrine's key from around her neck and placed it into the tiny keyhole at the bottom of the curved front concertina rollup door made from horizontal teak panels. "Ta! Daaah!" she cried out as it fitted perfectly and turned successfully with a sharp 'click'. Olive's dainty hands pulled the rollup panel front upwards. The desk was now completely opened with the contents fully on view.

Toby and Libby came across the room to stand stock-still in front of the desk, as Olive blew the rest of a coating of dust away that had been disturbed by her investigation.

"How quaint. It's the professor's old writing desk. What have you found in there, Olive?" asked her mum. With the covering sheet now completely discarded to one side, the writing desk appeared to be something more akin to a child's design rather than something more austere like the antique desk they had expected. This was a very basic rollup cabinet supported on four spindly metal tubular-shaped legs. However, Professor Greylag had seemingly made up for this with a splendid-looking high-back, black office chair, from which Olive had made herself comfortable during her examination of the newly discovered desk.

"Well, there's a notepad and pencil. I think I'll start my story. The story which Professor Greylag thought I could write!" she announced confidently. "There's an envelope in here also, Mum. I think you should read it. It's addressed to Professor Greylag. I'm sure he wouldn't mind though," she said respectfully, handing it over to her mum.

Olive listened eagerly as Libby read aloud the handwriting on the envelope.

*"Dear Professor Peregrine Greylag,*
*As you are well aware, since my generous agreement with you I have provided a continuous goodwill gesture to use part of the Didsvale Manor estate for your nature reserve and miniature railway. I regret to inform you that this generosity will now cease with immediate effect. My private surveyors have now advised me that not only has another sink hole appeared and in need of underpinning but the access bridge into the reserve crossing over the River Babble has unfortunately been assessed as structurally unsafe. Seeing as this bridge provides your miniature railway and walking visitors safe passage into the reserve, I must close this access with immediate effect. In the light of this news, I must cancel our agreement and look for a fitting alternative for the future prosperity of our village. I have consulted my surveyors and legal team and they have advised me that instead of costly and lengthy building of a new bridge, my financial investments would be better utilised for something that would bring new prosperity to us all in Didsvale. I wish you well for the future. Thank you for your help... in... this... matter. Yours... sincerely... Signed, Lord Didsvale, Tarquini Scumbali'."*

She finished reading hesitantly, in disgust at the obvious way the professor had been treated, and looked at Toby with incredulity. "Thank you for your help!" She repeated aloud. "How callous could he be to do such a horrible thing to Peregrine. Scumbali has really pulled the rug from under Peregrine's feet. In the blink of an eye, he lost his life's passions and then he lost his life!" Libby then continued with further alarm, "And hang on a second. What's to stop this nasty individual doing the same to us? Perhaps he's given us that generous short-term contract for a reason, as Captain Ahab suggested earlier! Maybe his ulterior motive was to keep us all nicely sweet for as long as possible as his Public Relations team. We would have foolishly kept telling all the villagers what a splendid landlord he was, while he gets on with his dastardly deeds. There's nothing to stop him from pulling the rug from under us in three months' time when we become surplus to his requirements and he kicks us out like he did with poor Professor Greylag. What about us? What about Kingfisher Cottage?" she added desperately, turning to Toby for support.

Toby stared back before adding to Libby's concerns. "And what if the professor's accident wasn't an accident after all? Maybe he found something out that he shouldn't. Perhaps he knew too much and someone didn't like it!"

Libby screwed up her face at the thought and nodded in shocked silent agreement at Toby's accusation. "We have to stop this Scumball of a Scumbali!" she insisted with continuous anger, before settling down to say profoundly, "I believe the name Tarquini comes from the last emperor of Rome, **or** Tarquini the Proud as he was allegedly called. Well,

Tarquini the Proud of Didsvale! Did you know that pride comes before a fall?"

"Absolutely," Toby agreed.

During the revealing exchange between her parents, Olive had kept her concentration and eyes focussed firmly on Peregrine's open writing desk, and began thoroughly examining something else. She had been completely oblivious to her mum's analysis of Tarquini's ultimatum letter to Peregrine. "I think I may have found your telescope, Mum?" Olive's hands raised above the desk presenting to her an oblong-shaped, highly polished teak box, with a shiny locking clasp at the front made of brass. On the side of the box, roughly carved out by hand was the wording '*Peregrine's Peeper*'.

Libby took the box carefully from Olive's grasp. "Oh. Thanks Olive. Look at this, he's written this funny inscription on the side. Yes! This could well be what I've been left in charge of. Let's see now." Upon which, she took hold of the key draped around her neck and offered it to the keyhole on the gleaming box she had balanced securely on top of the writing desk. Click! went the mechanism inside the box, indicating that this was the matching key. She slowly opened it to find the most exquisite antique telescope, gleaming in brass and silver. "Wow," she declared. "What a lovely object. Let's just take a closer look at you," she said in person to the object. Once extracted from the box, Libby noticed that a well-worn leather strap was attached to one end of the telescope. Taking the strap firstly she tenderly lifted the telescope from the box and pulled the end outwards section by section until it extended to its full length. She lifted Peregrine's antique specimen to one eye and commenced to look around the room until lining it up with Toby, standing there engrossed in the

110

revelation of his own key. "You could have had a shave this morning, Toby!" she said jokingly.

"Very funny!" he responded defensively. "I didn't have any time for a shave after you two hurried me here after rushing back from the manor house this morning."

"Only joking," Libby said apologetically before concentrating back onto the telescope at close quarters. "Ahab told us that Peregrine always carried this around with him everywhere he went, but for some strange reason he wasn't wearing it when he was found by the tree? Why would he have locked it away like this?" she mused further.

"Why indeed?" Toby agreed.

While Toby and Libby continued their dialogue, Olive was inspecting the clever design of the sliding concertina lid on the desk, mumbling repeatedly to herself the wording on the key label, "Seek and ye shall find, seek and ye shall find!" She'd taken the telescope box from the top of the desk and placed it back to the exact position where she'd found it inside. As she attempted to close the lid again it became jammed. Shaking it up and down in an attempt to release it, Olive gave out a relieved sigh as it finally freed itself and then delicately closed it back down. As she placed her key back again to lock it, something caught her eye. "What's this?" she inquired. Poking out of the narrow gap at the top of the lid at the point where it disappeared down the back of the desk, she kept the lid firmly shut and tenderly pulled the piece of paper gradually outwards, millimetre by millimetre, until an old postcard came entirely to view. Gripping her newly found discovery with one hand Olive used her other hand to raise the concertina lid back up again so she could lay the postcard down to look at it. Responding to her cry of surprise, Toby and Libby came back around to the front of the desk to peer over her shoulder to see what all the fuss was about. "Seek and I have found!" exclaimed Olive to herself as the postcard escaped her grip and fluttered to the floor.

Libby bent down, picked it up and studied it curiously. At first, she concentrated on one side, which had a lovely scenic coloured photograph printed on it. She immediately recognised that it was taken within the park and showed a scene of the old wooden railway bridge crossing the River Babble. Puffing its way across the bridge under a plume of smoke and steam, was a miniature steam train heading towards the nature reserve and Didsvale Manor. The river looked serene in the evening's summer sun with a single duck swimming peacefully downstream away from the bridge. The train was gleamingly polished and painted, predominately in apple green. The front of the train was festooned with flags. The carriages were decorated with drapes, flags, ribbons and banners. She could clearly see a familiar figure sat driving the steam engine and the joyful faces of dozens of passengers in the four tiny coaches being pulled behind it. "How enchanting!" she said to the others. "Look! It's a photograph of one of the old miniature steam trains crossing the bridge we saw earlier." She read the inscription printed along the bottom. "'OPENING CEREMONY—

THE FLYING COOTSMAN IN SUNSET OVER THE RIVER BABBLE—Copyright—Didsvale Park—4 August 1979', and look! I guess that man sitting in the cab driving the engine must be Professor Peregrine! You can't miss him with his coloured cap and gown. It looks as though he's sprouted wings in the train's backdraft. Awww! It's the Flying Cootsman, festooned for the day's celebrations. How sad that

Peregrine wasn't to know how badly things were going to turn out—and look how proud he looks on his special day? I don't know! What a crying shame!" she added sympathetically.

As she finished describing the souvenir postcard's scenic front, she turned it towards Toby for confirmation. "One thing I do know!" Toby answered.

"What's that?" replied Libby intrigued.

"I know how he took this picture! Just before I went across the river bridge into the reserve earlier, I noticed something catching the sun from inside a bat box that had been fixed high up onto a nearby tree. Well, I reckon that must be where Professor Peregrine installed a camera to capture this scene and many others at this setting."

"How clever," replied Libby. "I wonder how many others he took?"

"I've no idea, but I bet they sold well back at the souvenir shop," replied Toby.

Olive then noticed some wording on the reverse and pointed it out. "Mum, look! Turn it around. There's something written on the other side."

Libby turned the other side towards her and began to screw her face up to decipher the wording. "The handwriting's quite rough and barely legible. But I think it says…

'*Train your eye on this wonderful day, with me on the footplate of the Flying Cootsman at play. Crossing the river billowing smoke and steam with trout jumping below and maybe some bream. A feathered friend is a rare friend indeed, floating along for some supper to feed.*

*From where you stand look west to espy, my feathered friend to see again nearby.*'

"I presume Professor Peregrine wrote this strange conundrum," she suggested.

"I didn't know him, but looking at this I guess he liked the odd cryptic crossword now and again," surmised Toby. "Maybe he's playing a game with us?" he suggested.

Libby stepped in. "I do know that he thinks we are capable of keeping ahead of the game somehow by solving his riddles!" Toby momentarily opened his mouth to comment just as Libby halted him sharply to say. "And before you say it, Toby, I didn't mean that to be a 'game' bird pun either!" She began to screw her face up in deep concentration to make a suggestion. "I have a theory! Sometimes, it's better to resolve a problem by starting at the end and then working backwards. Olive! Will you stand in the centre of the room and find where due north is with your compass, please, and then point to where west is? You will see the method in your mother's madness!" she said calmly while placing a reassuring hand on Olive's shoulder.

Olive shot to where her mother had indicated and dug her compass out of her zip pocket and placed it flat into the palm of her hand. The compass hand began rotating around and around uncontrollably before slowing down and swivelling backwards and forwards, direction point by direction point, until it eventually stopped on a fixed position. Olive carefully placed her hand onto the outer rim of the compass and aligned the printed direction inside the glass cover, and with the arrow end of the compass hand settling on due north, she quickly calculated where west was. "There you are, Mum. West!" As she did so, all three looked towards the drawings on the wall in the direction of Olive's outstretched arm indicating to them where the west direction was.

Libby purposely grasped her recently acquired telescope from around her neck. She extended it to its full length, then brought it up to her eye and said jokingly in a pirate-style accent, "OK me hearties! What do we have here?" Then, using Olive's outstretched pointing arm to navigate her with, kept peering up and down the opposite wall full of Peregrine's sketches before striding across the room to stand by the arc of the wall where Olive's arm was pointing to. She grasped the postcard firmly in her other hand switching her concentration frequently from the postcard to the wall, up and down and then side to side repeatedly until arriving at the exact point of her examination, then began speaking like a detective describing a crime scene. "Right. Now we've arrived at due west as it hints in the rhyme. What do we see on the postcard? We see a lovely scene, depicting Peregrine on the footplate of the Flying Cootsman. '*Train your eye*' Peregrine starts by saying. Mmmm. Is that a clue? No that's just to test us! Because, on examining the evidence here at due west, there are numerous bird drawings." She continued looking at the detail on the postcard, announcing her finding to Toby and Olive, both listening alertly with furrowed brows attempting to keep up with her detective work. She carried on squinting at the postcard, trying to decipher each word. "'*A feathered friend is a rare friend indeed, floating along for some supper to feed.*' She flipped the postcard back over to study the picture once again. "Mmmmm. Aah! Of course! What do we have here?" she declared. "What we have here is a lovely 'rare' specimen gliding along the river, and if I'm not mistaken this lovely 'rare' specimen is otherwise known as a **smew**!" She diverted her attention back to the wall and began searching up and down it, repeating some of the words from the rhyme as she did so. "So, where are you, my rare feathered friend floating along for some supper to feed? Ah! Voila. We have our main suspect!" she cried out dramatically and victoriously. Midway up the wall amongst the many other bird drawings, the end of Libby's finger could be seen connecting with the unmistakable and distinctive colourful sketch of a **smew** duck. She pulled it from its fixed position on the wall and held it aloft for the others to see.

"Oh, well done, Miss Marple!" Toby cried, clapping his hands.

Olive joined in. "Yes, Mum. Now it's your turn to be super sleuth," she added proudly.

"And we all know what this means?" Libby said intriguingly.

Toby's eyes lit up at the realisation of what she was inferring to, before answering with astonishment, "It means that our Peregrine is leading us to another rare **smew**. His SMEW squawk box!"

Libby and Olive took on their own astonished expressions with mouths agape before Libby added humorously. "Oh, that was very well worked out Inspector Morse... Code! But we must move onto our next case..." Libby said impatiently before adding... "which is this!" She then flipped over the newly discovered picture of the smew and thrust it forwards for the others to see. "Look, yet another conundrum! Peregrine certainly knows how to keep you in suspense. And how to test your eyesight!" she quipped while studying intensely at Peregrine's erratic handwriting. "Well, we're definitely not on a wild goose chase but more like a secret 'smew' chase!" she quipped humorously.

"Oh. Nice one, Libby. OK. What clue do we have now?" asked Toby eagerly.

"This is a little more mysterious. It's another cryptic one. I'll give it my best shot. Here goes!" she said in anticipation before reciting again. As she did so, her hand began to shake in surprise and her voice took on a more serious, incredulous tone as her voice began to quiver...

"'*The Adamsons are almost there with fearless nature and without despair! Three letters of my name have a point to make but the odd one out you alter...*

*...for the key to this quest of my precious possession is somewhere around, don't falter! So press on firmly and stay on track to the very end and don't look back!*'"

After composing herself, Libby addressed the others with disbelief at the mention of their name in the text. "Peregrine knew we were coming to find the SMEW! How on earth was he able to know our name?" she queried. "He's never met us!"

"Maybe he has though, Mum!" Olive began to offer her mind-blowing explanation. "Maybe it was with the power of his brainwaves and second sight before his accident? Remember the murmuration message?"

At which point, Libby's jaw dropped open and in a semi-dazed state said, "Wow Olive. That's some theory. Let's hold that thought though and try to crack on!"

Toby stepped in and prised the smew sketch from Libby's clenched hand as she stood motionless in shock. "Let me take that," he offered helpfully. "Sit down and rest your brain for a minute. Let me have a crack at this one." He looked down at the wording on the back of the sketch and repeated it again to himself under his breath. With Libby now recovered and fully attentive, both she and Olive concentrated on Toby's somewhat deliberate, pompous interpretation of Peregrine's second conundrum, as though he was presiding in a courtroom. He began. "Right! Let's look at the evidence. It's obvious here that Peregrine knew us by some means or other. In that respect the jury is still out! We have found his **smew** duck so I presume that we are getting very close to finding his SMEW Squawkerlingo machine. I'm reading his directions very carefully and can offer the following conclusion. '*Three letters of my name have a point to make but the odd one out you alter!*' I can confirm that the three letters of *my name*, **Smew,** are **making out** true compass directions. That's 'S' for south, 'E' for east and 'W' for west," he spelt out each phonetically. "That leaves the letter 'M' as the odd one out." His shrewd deduction then seemed to grind to a halt as he pondered for a few seconds before suddenly declaring. "The letter M '*does alter*' and therefore *does alter* from the letter 'M' to the missing direction, which is 'N' for North! And according to this first line we need to find due north. But from where?" He pondered for a moment then repeated part of the line as a question, "…'*treasured possession* and *somewhere around and near*'?"

Olive made a suggestion. "Could '*around and* near' mean somewhere near to his treasured possession being the Flying Cootsman, which is above us in the roundhouse?"

"By jove I think she's got it. Yes! That's it, Olive. Well done. We need to go back up and look inside the roundhouse. Let's go."

As the three made their way back up the steps into the roundhouse, Toby continued with his deduction. "Olive. Will you go and do the same thing again with your compass but this time find the due north direction from the centre of the turntable please, but be careful," he added caringly.

"Yes. Watch how you go," added Libby protectively.

Olive sprang up the ladder onto the turntable and worked her way to the centre before holding her compass steadily once again in her open palm. She waited for the compass pointer to go through its wild fluctuations and rotations again before settling onto the capital letter 'N' to confirm due north. She repositioned herself until lining up with where the compass arrow was indicating where to go. "There you go, Dad. Due north! It's directly in line with that turntable track over there!"

"OK, you can both come over now." Toby had already started to follow Olive's compass direction to arrive exactly at the position where the Flying Cootsman was stabled. "Here we are. Due north!" He raised the postcard once more to eye-level and began to read out a few more words of the professor's riddle. "'… *my precious possession and key to this quest is somewhere around, don't falter.*' Aha! Well, you were right with 'around', Olive. He means 'around' as in 'a' **roundhouse**. We've also found 'N' for north and his *precious possession*, The Flying Cootsman! But where is that damn elusive SMEW?" he added in frustration. "And, what does he mean by 'key to this quest'?" At this juncture, he suddenly noticed that the postcard's edge had caught the key strap draped around his neck. He lifted it out to read the label attached to the key. The wording immediately caught his eye, which he began to read aloud. "'*Appearances Deceive*'!" he yelled at the others. "Yes! That's it! Look here, written on the back of my key that the professor trusted me with. '*Appearances Deceive!*'" He turned the key label to show the others in an attempt to convince them where his thinking was coming from. "I think we're getting very warm—very, very warm! Almost as warm as this beautiful steam engine's boiler will be again one day, I hope! If I'm not mistaken, Peregrine is telling us that the Flying Cootsman isn't just a steam engine, but something else as well!" he emphasised. "This is obviously his *'precious possession!'*" he pointed out while referring to the first unresolved part of the line, then hesitated for a few seconds as Libby and Olive looked on perplexed. He read out the last line of the rhyme. "'*So press on firmly and stay on track to the very end and don't look back.*' Right. Let's see where this takes us, Toby!" He was now on a personal mission, talking to himself as he read the line, slowly breaking it down phrase by phrase.

Libby interjected. "Why don't you try using my technique and mix the wording up back to front? That's sometimes a good way to solve cryptic clues."

"OK. Good thinking. Let's try this bit," he suggested, "'*Stay on track to the very end and don't look back!*'" he read out. Toby adhered to Libby's shrewd advice and started to walk along the side of the gleaming engine until he reached the buffer stop at the end. Libby and Olive followed his every footstep right up to the engine buffer. "OK. Now what? So much for that theory, Libby," he said sarcastically. "How on earth can we **press on** when we're at the end of the track?"

While her parents were debating the clues, Olive peered between the two of them and grabbed the postcard from Toby's hand then looked at it and shouted, "Like this, Dad!" She stretched out her hand towards the name plaque **'ONE— FLYING COOTSMAN'**, and then firmly pressed the letters 'O' and 'N' of the word 'ONE' simultaneously together with two of her fingers. The letters responded by receding back into the name plaque until they couldn't go any further, before slowly and silently rebounding back to their original position, completing word 'ONE' again. "There you. 'Press **ON**'! Easy!" she added proudly to her father before placing the postcard safely protected in her dungaree pocket for safe keeping and tapping it victoriously as she did so.

"That was fantastic, Ol…" Toby was cut off just as he was about to concede to Olive's ingenuity, but was interrupted by a surprising quiet hissing noise. "What's that noise?" he asked the others.

"I've no idea," Libby replied as the hissing slowly began to get louder and louder. "Err! I think may have done something wrong!" Olive admitted scarily.

"No, you haven't, Olive. Somehow, I think you may have done something very, very right!" added Libby, now equally surprised as the three huddled together shaking with fright while the deafening hissing was joined by a jet of steam coming from around the front wheels of the engine. As the hissing got louder, more and more steam hissed from out of the Flying Cootsman's pistons, and completely enveloped them until they couldn't see a thing. Suddenly, there was a loud, thunderous, grating noise of metal on metal, which seemed to them to go on for an eternity. Then, the hissing slowly diminished until there was complete silence again. The steam began to evaporate around them, slowly snaking upwards before disappearing through the air vent above. As it did so, the Adamsons were able to see clearly around the roundhouse shed once again. Except now, they noticed that something quite extraordinary had happened as they stood there with mouths agape at the scene. The Flying Cootsman had mysteriously moved forwards from its stabled position to stand motionless in the centre of the turntable. The only other evidence of its ghostly movement was a slight trickle of water coming from a narrow pipe attached to a box above one of its wheels.

Toby stood there shocked with amazement, trying to rationalise the situation. "Now, that's what I 'literally' call moving under your own steam. How on earth did that happen? I wonder why she's moved into that particular position?" He scratched his head in bemusement.

"It happened when Olive resolved the bit in the clue about 'pressing on firmly' and pressed the letters ON firmly!" answered Libby, now recomposed. "Didn't you, Olive, you clever cookie? Olive? Olive?" she repeated with growing concern. "Where's that child disappeared to now?" she added, her worry now obviously growing at Olive's sudden departure who was nowhere to be seen.

"Under here! I'm under the turntable again! You'll never guess what I'm looking at though?" came a familiar voice shouting with excitement from underneath the turntable. Olive had bolted back unnoticed to Peregrine's underground study while her parents were discussing the ghostly goings-on together by the turntable. Toby and Libby hurried back from the turntable and almost slid down the steps into the study to find Olive sitting on a small seat attached to the front of the strangest contraption they had ever seen. They got there just in time to see two small sections of miniature railway track disconnecting themselves from both sides of the contraption. Then with the assistance of a number of connecting chains, cogs and pulleys, slid smoothly and effortlessly upwards through the open ceiling door hatch. As the hatch was closing they could see the pieces of track automatically locking into position from where they came from, directly underneath the Flying Cootsman above. Just as the hatch door was reclosing, they could clearly make out the gaping hole inside the Flying Cootsman's boiler where the contraption was housed, before somehow it mysteriously opened and lowered itself into the study below. Olive had arrived to see a small section of the boiler's outer casing opening out to reveal some kind of musical keyboard, and then mechanically unravelling a small, extended seat on which she now sat staring at the keyboard, analysing the content of the newly hatched arrival. Attaching the seat to the machine, were a row of long wooden foot pedals, which Olive could just about reach with her feet. Except this was no ordinary keyboard! There were three ascending rows of keys, but instead of them having traditional black and white keys, these each contained individual letters and strange markings on a silver background. She suddenly noticed her astonished parents standing behind her and announced. "May I introduce Professor Peregrine Greylag's masterpiece invention…!" and then hesitated before taking a dramatic deep breath and bellowing out… "His **SMEW, Squawkbox** machine!"

"Ta Daaaah!" she declared by theatrically sweeping her hand across the front of the weird object right in front of her for extra dramatic effect. "Squawkerlingo, here we go! go! go," she added humorously.

Toby stood in complete fascination, taking in the new addition to Peregrine's study since they were last there just a few short minutes since. Once his examination had finished, he began to relay his finding to the others but not before he spoke directly to the contraption. "So, here you are, Peregrine's '*Deceptive Appearance*'," he confirmed, with reference to the wording on his key label. "So now we have finally found you!" He then redirected the confirmation of his engineering prowess findings back to Libby and Olive, pointing at each part of his deductions as he went along starting with the newly discovered SMEW machine. "Oh, I see. How ingenious. It looks like it has descended through the bottom of the turntable into the study from inside Flying Cootsman's boiler through the open hatch door in the ceiling. Then, it's been guided down with the help of two small pieces of track and pulleys from the turntable above, splitting into two equal sections. They, in turn, have interlocked with those four wheels on the side of SMEW, which have cleverly guided it down into the study by some kind of elaborate pneumatic system inside the boiler. This has left the SMEW in position; balanced on those four tiny round pipes acting as supporting legs to balance on, the track pieces have retracted back to where they came from and reconnected on the turntable. Then, as if by magic, the ceiling hatch reclosed again as if this thing has appeared out of nowhere. Without doubt, an absolute engineering masterpiece," he concluded, with his technical pronouncement and testimony to Professor Peregrine's brilliance. "This weird specimen of a machine now takes up position in the centre of the study where he could carry out his secretive projects completely out of sight to any prying eyes. It would never be out of his sight. Yes. I conclude that the Flying Cootsman is actually Professor Peregrine Greylag's magnificent SMEW machine in disguise. WOW!"

Olive, who was still trying to work the keyboard's strange arrangement markings and oblivious to her father's pontificating, began to touch some of the keys. Libby noticed what she was doing. "Olive! Don't touch anything just yet, please. Let your dad have a look. He's the one qualified to decipher this. He's the expert on trains and engineering and also likes a good cryptic puzzle."

However, Libby's advice was too late for Olive to respond to as she was already pressing separately the keys containing the letters S, M, E, and W, which she'd located around the keyboard. As she depressed the last letter, clicking noises could be heard from inside the casing. Olive jumped from her seat and stood back with her parents in anticipation of what was happening within the SMEW machine.

They watched in fascination as the black metal section just above the keyboard slid upwards before disappearing down into the back of the casing, revealing a small narrow ledge above the keyboard that traditionally held pieces of music. Instead of a piece of music sitting on the ledge, they could see a piece of a white notepad beginning to gradually appear until the words 'SMEW—OPERATOR'S MANUAL' came into full view. Also coming into view further up was a panel of instruments and an integrated glass fronted box with a long horizontal slot positioned immediately beneath it. To one side of the box was a warning gauge with the label '*magicmunchymulch level*', signifying that the amount was at no more than a few droplets the way its marker had entered the 'danger nearly empty' section, and signified by a flashing red warning light glowing above it. A notelet was stuck to one side with the wording '*smew programming completed*' written on it. On the other side of the console was a similar sticky notelet containing the same scruffy handwriting, '*S. D. M.*'

— *R & D—must only be used in emergency for happy memory assistance!*'

A row of thirteen silver music pipes of various sizes had

risen from inside the casing and stood fixed in a row along the top. Each pipe contained a letter spelling out the word S.Q.U.A.W.K.E.R.L.I.N.G.O. As this section of the machine completed its manoeuvre, two separate doors sprang open sideways before some hidden hinges clicked them into fixed positions. Each door was covered with an assortment of familiar organ stops, except the handles of them all had been beautifully decorated with illustrations of bird species. Just below the music ledge was a row of sliver flick switches with a different set of abbreviations written underneath them all. To one side of the pipes could be seen a small funnel protruding upwards.

With the SMEW machine seemingly completely unravelled, Toby cautiously approached it and squirmed into position on the seat Olive had previously vacated with such hurry. He addressed its absent inventor and grabbed the instruction manual from its position. As he did so, a small compass face embedded into the wooden panel came into view from behind. "Mmmm and what other oddity is this, Professor Peregrine Greylag? Not just a traditional printed compass face, but a glass compass face with a line roughly drawn onto it with a marker pen with the abbreviation S.S.W.R.? This must be his mythical direction point."

"Yes, Dad. South by south-west recurring!" shouted out Olive. "And it isn't mythical. It's true, otherwise he wouldn't have written it on the glass!" she insisted. "And look at that sticky note. 'S.D.M.—R & D'. I bet those initials stand for Silver... Dream... Machine, which is the other project that Ahab said the professor was working on!"

"Yes! Of course it is. Well worked out, Olive," said Libby. "And R and D will stand for 'research and development'."

"Well, this whole invention's a real show-stopper if you ask me! What, with all these beautifully illustrated organ stops!" Toby quipped before continuing. "Right Peregrine our dear friend. Let's see what mysteries you have left us to unfold!" as he started to thumb through the pages of the operator's manual.

Libby spoke out after a short while with deliberate exaggeration, after taking stock of the incredible new revelation. "So, SMEW is the old Lord Didsvale's pipe organ, but slightly refurbished! How absolutely amazing!"

"Except this is nothing like your traditional mini pipe organ now!" joined in Toby, momentarily diverting his eyes from the manual and declaring with excitement, "This is now something more like Professor Peregrine Greylag's excellent *Squawkerlingo Migration Encryption Worldwide*—**SMEW** machine! I agree with you two. Let's ignore the yellow sticky note labelled 'S.D.M.—R and D' for now. Unfortunately, his Research and Development will have to wait till another day. First things first, let's just concentrate on SMEW for now."

For the next few minutes, Toby read through the manual, only to interrupt his concentration by touching and confirming the location of each part in accordance with the manual's guidance. Libby and Olive used up this time to examine the machine from all sides until Toby ended his studying with a confirmation. "Well, OK it seems like it's all been programmed and the controls are pretty straightforward too— in an unbelievably, fantastical, mind blowing, straightforward, kind of way! We've got everything needed to communicate with any bird, to and from any place in the world. In a nutshell, we carry on with the professor's work and hopefully give him the accolade he deserves for his discovery and invention.

There's no mention of those switches, so we had better not touch them." He looked at them and began to query, "I wonder what they mean though, R.B.B.B.B... N.R.B.B...?"

Libby interrupted his thoughts before he carried on. "I think you've done enough thinking for now."

Toby repositioned the manual back onto the ledge where he found it and then suggested, "Yes, you're right. I think we should all get some fresh air and go for a walk along the river and back." He pressed the keyboard letters S.M.E.W. and watched as the machine slowly folded back in on itself with just the keyboard left in position. "Pure genius!" he confirmed as the machine made its ultimate closing click. "However, the magicmunchymulch fuel is down to the last drops so let's hope Captain Ahab returns soon with more supplies."

The three made their way to the ladder hatch when Libby said. "We left the hatch open. I'm not sure Peregrine would have approved of that oversight!" One by one, they climbed back out onto the turntable and walked towards the door.

"Just as well that rascal Scumbali isn't around to spoil the pa..." Before Toby could finish his sentence, it was abruptly stopped by another voice booming loudly from the engine shed door. Libby and Olive stood looking immediately from behind where Toby stood, mouth agape with fear. With the fading sunshine behind him, the uninvited silhouette standing in the engine shed doorway stepped forward to take on a more familiar appearance.

"Well, if it's not the grizzly Adamson family!" the silhouette announced, before continuing, "...spoil the what, may I ask?" Tarquini Scumbali glared at Toby, prompting him to complete his sentence but rudely finished it on his behalf anyway... "Party by any chance? Yes, all four of us are definitely going to have a party! Oh! How I do love a good party." He then laughed maniacally at his sinister intimidation before continuing to address the surprised Adamsons. "It's amazing how much voices amplify around this building, especially from that mad professor's secret little den down there I saw you all appearing from. What a wonderful auditorium. You seem to have a very special machine down there. I knew that mad professor was up to something and it was such a pity that he never had the chance to complete his work before his dreadful accident." Tarquini started to goad them with deliberate insensitivity and sarcasm. So much that it forced Toby to retaliate.

"What do you mean by that? You know more about the professor's accident than you care to admit, don't you?" He said accusingly.

"How dare you make such an insinuation? I was nowhere near his blasted accident. That, I can assure you! I was making a call from the manor house to a close friend, who will easily be able to corroborate my story. I'm certain there'll be a record of that for the police to check out should you so wish," Tarquini retaliated defensively. "Why don't you Adamsons stop droning on and on and on!"

Libby, who had been listening to the sentences coming from Tarquini's lips and scowling at every word, suddenly opened her face up wide with surprise as he gave out an unintentional clue to the strange goings-on at Didsvale Manor, which she had leapt on straight away.

Tarquini noticed her reaction. "And what's surprised you, Mrs Busybody! Sneaking around my manor grounds with your little brat!" he said rudely.

"Don't you speak to us like that," jumped in Olive, aiming

a kick at one of Tarquini's shins.

Libby held her back. "It's OK, poppet. I'm sure Mr Scumbali will get what he deserves in time!

"Whatever!" replied Scumbali dismissively. "Anyway, when you've heard why I'm here maybe you'll see some sense and be nice to me after all. I'm going to ask a little favour from you. I think, firstly, you should all listen very carefully to what I have to say or your friend Captain Ahab may find himself in somewhat... how should I put it? How about... somewhat deep and dangerous hot waters!" he said threateningly.

"What do you mean by deep and dangerous waters? What have you done with our friend?" pleaded Olive.

"Oh, don't worry, young lady. I haven't done anything with your friend. Yet! But that depends, doesn't it?" replied Scumbali.

"Depends on what?" Libby broke in. "Don't speak to my daughter like that. Why don't you pick on someone your own size? And where's that Italian accent disappeared to, you! ... you! Conna Manna!" She couldn't help but deliver this insulting blow to Tarquini once it was realised that his fake Italian accent had changed to something more suited to a thick southern English dialect. Toby and Olive sniggered together at the joke.

Tarquini quickly turned his attention back to the Adamsons. "What do you think you pair are laughing at?" At which point Toby and Olive took on more serious expressions again. "I listened in to almost every word he spoke to you at his Bosun's squalor place yesterday."

"It's his Cabin! Bosun's Cabin!" Olive corrected Tarquini emphatically.

"Whatever!" retorted Tarquini. "Anyway, I have

photographic evidence that your desperate captain stole one of my most valuable antiques from Didsvale Manor and the moment he steps back on shore, all I have to do is call the police to have him locked up! But you don't really want that to happen, do you?" he said, giving the Adamsons no alternative.

Libby turned to Toby and shrugged her shoulders, who responded with the same defeated gesture, then acting as spokesperson, turned to face Tarquini and answered resignedly, "OK, what exactly is it you want us to do to help with your evil plan?"

"Evil plan, you say. This is no evil plan!" he replied sarcastically. "Let's just say we're entering a business negotiation to help each other in the longer term. This is what I wish you to do. I've already told you how much I enjoy a good party. Well, this evening there is a special garden party being held at Didsvale Village Hall, and yours truly, the much revered and respected Lord Didsvale, has been asked to make personal presentations at Didsvale's fancy Garden fete. This year marks the centenary anniversary of the presentation and I have personally funded the purchase of a special brand new, and highly valuable, solid silver trophy for this year's 'Life Time Achievement Award' to mark the occasion. As a kind gesture in return, the village councillors have asked me to present the award!" He paused to take in some more personal adulation. "Oh, how Didsvale's villagers love their benefactor. Certainly more than a new goody two-shoes family, coming into the village!" he remarked in such a cynical way to belittle the Adamsons. "Anyway, here is what I want you to do. Get a pen and some paper!" he demanded.

"I'll get some from the writing desk," Olive offered.

"OK, but no clever stuff, smarty pants Adamson!" he aimed at Olive in particular, who scampered across the engine shed to Peregrine's study and back again to hand him a pencil and a piece of blank paper. Tarquini shouted at Toby. "You! Mr Snoopy Adamson! Copy this down and feed these coordinates and these instructions into that clever machine of yours and then let me have it back." He handed Toby his own bit of scribbled paper.

Toby breathed in deeply at the shock of what he was being ordered to do in collateral for Ahab's safety. He then gave Tarquini's original piece of paper back to him, which he folded carefully and placed inside his jacket pocket. "You'll never get away with this. We can't do that!" he pleaded.

"Oh, yes, I will, and yes you will!" insisted Scumbali. "So here's the deal. You carry out your side of this bargain and I promise that you'll be off the hook completely. All you need to do afterwards is to leave the village permanently. If you try to be clever, I'll simply use all the evidence I have to incriminate you all and so be answerable to the courts, along with your friend, Captain Seasick! Just think of the dreaded consequences for your heroic captain! He'll need lots of sailor's rum to go with his prison porridge if you don't comply!" he sniggered. "You can all go back to where you came from and leave Didsvale Village in peace, and I promise on my father's grave that you and your beloved captain will be off the hook and will be as free as the birds on my wonderful estate." He checked himself for a second before adding, "Oh! I nearly forgot in my pure excitement that there are a couple of other little conditions to our special arrangement before I leave you, my good friends. Firstly, I must ask you to cover that old empty coal storage bunker outside with that and stretch it as tightly as you can." At which point, Tarquini pointed to a piece of green mesh netting next to the old railway coal box he'd placed there earlier. "Well, go on you, get it sorted, Mrs Snoopy Adamson!" he said rudely as he pointed to Libby, prompting her to do his deed, which she did with a huff before returning back inside the shed.

He then addressed Toby. "And secondly. You, Mr Snoopy Adamson! Give me the key to this place." Toby reluctantly dragged the key from around his neck and threw it at Tarquini, who just managed to catch it.

"Now, now! Temper, temper, Mr Snoopy! Let's all be friends for the best outcome for all," Tarquini said snidely.

Olive suddenly burst forward and embraced Tarquini. "Please don't harm our friend, Captain Ahab. He's not done you any harm. I didn't really mean to kick out at you, Lord Tarquini!"

"Back off, bratty Adamson!" responded Tarquini angrily, while pushing her away towards her mother, who took her hand and pulled her safely closer to her side.

"That was a bit over the top and melodramatic. Are you OK?" Libby whispered to Olive.

"Never been so good," Olive replied out of the side of her mouth. Libby looked back at her very perplexed.

Tarquini went on. "As you can see from my wonderful attire, I'm 'suited and booted' for the village garden party awards to make my presentations and fulfil my alibi in a few hours. You will invoke my orders at seven thirty precisely, without fail, and I will see you later. As an opera lover, I can't help but see the irony of some of the lines from the Beggar's Opera—'*A covetous fellow, like a jackdaw, steals what he was never made to enjoy, for the sake of hiding it.*' Anyway—Must fly!" At which, Tarquini stepped backwards through the engine shed door before locking it behind him and darting away back towards the river bridge, and the safety of Didsvale Manor. Laughing uncontrollably as he went, The Adamsons could just about hear his last sarcastic rhetorical question and answer to himself as he shouted from the distance. "And do you know what the word for a group of jackdaws is, my dear family Adamsons? A train! Ha! Ha! Ha! Haaaaaah. A train!"

As the Adamsons slowly recomposed themselves, Libby pressed her finger firmly to her lips, indicating that they should stay silent. She began to indicate with her index finger where she wanted Toby and Olive to follow, which was back to Peregrine's underground soundproof study. Libby closed the hatch after the other two had entered and began to speak quietly, "This place is soundproof, remember? I wanted to get us all here where we can't be heard in case he's still listening outside. I think I may know how he's been able to snoop on us so easily, by the way. And it's not Ditty Dotty! He's nothing but an out and out confidence trickster getting this village to dance to his operatic tunes! What a horrible specimen!"

"What exactly do you mean?" Toby replied.

"Drones! Could he be doing all of this with drones? Sounds a bit far-fetched but he's always so confident about what he knows. How does he know so much and do so much? When Scumbali said inadvertently we were 'droning' on, it made me think."

Toby closed his eyes in deep concentration at Libby's detective work before concurring with her. "Of course. There's nothing far-fetched about modern technology these days. I've seen all kinds of drones being flown around the place. There're no bounds to what they can be used for these days. Tarquini

Scumbali may have made his first mistake!" With one hand stroking his face in further thought and the other tightly grasping Scumbali's written instructions, he began to walk slowly around the study, continuing with his deductions as he went. "How was he able to listen into our conversation at Bosun's Cabin? How did he know that we were here in the engine shed? You said that the first letter on that hidden sticker on the truck you came across at Didsvale Manor was a letter 'D'! What was that strange whirring noise I could hear reverberating inside that underground cavern on the nature reserve earlier? What did he use to cover the trees with netting so quickly and evicting the wildlife from their homes as a result? What took the 'photographic evidence' pictures of Ahab?" Toby came to a sudden halt on his frantic circular walkabout and stood frozen with a look of shock and realisation on his face. "And more to the point, what if those four circular marks that Ahab noticed on the ground near to the crestfallen Professor weren't part of one of his experiments after all. What if that last word Ahab couldn't make out from Peregrine's lips just as he passed away stood for... What did he say... 'deadly dro...'!" He stared at the others who had taken in every single word and arrived together at the same conclusion as they announced as one... "Drones!"

Toby continued. "Unfortunately, we have no proof that drones had anything to do with Peregrine's accident, which puts Scumbali well in the clear. I wouldn't be surprised if he's used them to spy on every single committee member and is blackmailing them. And as for Dotty D'eath? Well, maybe she quite likes the prospect of becoming the next Lady Didsvale? I wouldn't put it past the deluded old bat. Anyway, let's put all of this to one side and dance to his tune for now. Speaking of tunes, this is the tune he wants us to play on this old pipe organ, otherwise known as SMEW, at seven thirty tonight."

He handed the instructions to Libby, who scanned it to herself before looking aghast, saying! "So, he's also got his perfect alibi for tonight from most of Didsvale's villagers! We must concentrate on these instructions and hold our nerve." Then, placing their hands together, they recited their family motto. *"Through all weathers the Adamsons will try, then onwards and upwards they will fly!"*

# Chapter 12
# The Garden Party

Didsvale village hall, with its manicured front lawn and multi-coloured flowerbeds, looked immaculate. The hall was festooned with bunting and a banner draped from the guttering displaying the bright coloured wording... *'Didsvale Village-Centenary Garden Party & Best Kept Garden Awards 2020'*

The rear garden was laid out with dozens of tables and chairs, each full with local residents, all dressed in their finery with many using the occasion to wear their best jewellery. Suspended from tall bushes surrounding the garden, were lines of solar lights, waiting for the later dusk to start displaying their charming multi-coloured glowing effects. Directly in front of the patio doors leading from the hall, was a separate table with two chairs placed facing the garden. A sign had been placed upon it stating '**RESERVED—HEAD JUDGE AND GUEST**'. The unmistakable outline of a large trophy covered with a red velvet cloth was hidden away under the table. On top of the table was a much more modest smaller trophy, hidden under a plain paper napkin along with three overturned certificates, similarly hidden from view of any over-anxious impatient participants. There was a distinct air of anticipation, made evident by the nervous chatter and laughter adding to the atmosphere of the attendees who were awaiting the appearance of the overdue Lord Didsvale, Tarquini Scumbali, to present the awards. Council leader, Dotty D'eath, was mingling with her fellow councillors and the general public before her phone vibrated to show Tarquini's incoming signal confirming his arrival. She made her apologies and made her way hurriedly inside the hall to meet Tarquini in a small anti-room. They quickly acknowledged each other with air kisses before Tarquini quickly locked the door behind them and began to speak. He held her wrists with both his hands, staring directly into her transfixed eyes. "My dear Dotty, our master plan is working as beautifully as your intoxicating perfume is on me at this moment! However, we must keep our composure and very soon I'll be holding the hands of the next Lady Didsvale!" Dotty stared into his hypnotic eyes with excitement as he went on. "Our obstacles are gradually being swept aside one by one. We got rid of that prying professor for good. That ridiculous nautical nasty, Captain Ahab McCrab, will soon be back from his high seas and directly into deep water with my ingenious set-up with the police, and soon the pesky Adamsons will soon be convicted criminals and driven out of the village with shame! Go! Quickly Dotty and make your grand entrance to your worshipping subjects. But remember our plan. You must finish the awards a few minutes before seven thirty!" Dotty nodded vigorously in agreement to her instructions like a nodding Labrador puppy. Tarquini's flattering remarks were food and drink to her ego as he unlocked the door to allow her to sweep majestically by and back out into the garden. She acknowledged various respectful nods from around the garden before taking her seat at the reserved table, where she temporarily sat checking that everything was in place. Once this was completed, it was now for Dotty D'eath to perform her most celebrated announcements to the villagers of

Didsvale. Making a repetitive, tapping, clinking noise with her gold writing pen onto her champagne glass, she rose from her chair smiling broadly to the garden party gathering as she did so. "Dearest proud villagers of Didsvale, welcome to this wonderful event on such a sunny, balmy evening. I am humbled to be here today to present these awards both as your council leader and Head Judge of our prestigious 'Best Kept Garden' competition. I'm even more humbled that this year marks the one hundredth anniversary of this event and that I have the personal privilege in being your parish council leader on this auspicious occasion. Because this is such a special occasion, we wanted to have an extra special award to commemorate it with. This will soon be presented by our generous village benefactor and sponsor of this award, who has asked me to apologise to you for his running late. Apparently, he found an abandoned puppy on his estate today and had to wait for the dog's home miles away from here to come and rescue it. However, all is well. So, now that he has finally made it, may I please ask you to put your warm hands together for our very own Lord Didsvale, Tarquini Scumbali." Dotty's arm signalled towards the patio doors where Tarquini had been waiting for his cue out of sight. Upon hearing this, he bounded through the doors like a TV game show host milking his eager audience. The rapturous applause died down as he settled into his seat, beckoning to the garden party guests as he did so with a modest hand gesture to end their adulation. He endeared himself further to the gathering by referring to his canine heroics by making movements with his hands like a dog begging its owner for forgiveness. This resulted in smatterings of laughter from the villagers. Dotty continued. "Welcome, Lord Scumbali. We're so glad that you finally made it after your earlier charitable deed to present these awards this evening. But firstly, I have an extra special announcement to make on behalf of Didsvale Parish Council. It is an announcement that will provide prosperity for every resident in this amazing village for today's generations and for generations to come." She looked over at one particular table where the Chief Reporter for the Didsvale Dynamo newspaper, Nellie Buchanan, sat looking on intensely. "Please have your editorial scribe at the ready for this scoop, Nellie," Dotty advised the ambitious reporter. "Today we unanimously voted to accept Lord Scumbali's exciting and futuristic proposal to build an eco-friendly energy facility on the old reserve. As you are aware, the reserve has been inaccessible due to dangerous sink holes and this will be a way to make full use of it again for us all. Each household of Didsvale will receive free electricity and furthermore, each will be entitled to shares dividend payments when the excess energy is sold back to the national grid!" Nellie Buchanan went into overdrive with her freshly sharpened pencil to scribble away furiously into her opened notebook. Each and every person looked around in all directions, giving instant approval expressions to each other at Dotty's ground-breaking announcement before breaking into spontaneous applause. Tarquini Scumbali held his head high with his nose pointing smugly upwards, nodding appreciatively at the ecstatic response from every table. The applause reached its crescendo and then died down into a respectful silence as Dotty D'eath continued in full gushing flow, "Well! After that wonderful response we can now get down to the process of announcing the result of our Best Kept Garden competition. In third place is Wally Walker of Duck Pond View!" The villagers clapped respectfully as Wally looked a tad disappointed, but still ambled up grumpily to receive a handshake and to collect his certificate from Dotty. "In second place, Pauline and Giles Perbrett of Four Seasons Cottage!" The clapping continued enthusiastically as the Perbretts turned to each other with pride as Pauline trotted up to Dotty, received her platitudes and returned to show Mr Perbrett the certificate award for their gardening exploits. "And finally, in first place and the winner of Didsvale's Best Kept Garden, Twenty-Twenty, is…" and then with a pause as long as a TV host holding back the winner's result to tantalise the audience for extra drama, she boomed. "…Mary and Eddie Shinroar of Holly Bush Mews!" The Shinroars shouted with glee at the result and came rushing forward to the continuing applause, which had now increased in volume for the popular victors. Dotty unveiled the winner's trophy and handed it to the Shinroars, who proudly picked out their names inscribed on it. They accepted the tiny trophy and held it aloft with a shared little finger each, and grabbed their certificate to the loudest round of applause so far. "Well done to our green-fingered gardeners, Mary and Eddie, who are also our revered local opticians. How ironic that you are the twenty-twenty winners. We can see you always had your sights on this award with your professional twenty-twenty vision!" Dotty rounded off the Best Kept Village awards with some out-of-character nervous puns and tittered away with the sycophantic audience as the victors returned to their seats. Tarquini, deliberately tapping his watch to indicate the precise time, caught her eye. He lifted four fingers to indicate how many minutes were left to conclude her final presentation, before the seven thirty deadline. Without hesitation, at his subtle prompt, Dotty boomed across the garden, "AND last, but **very** not least, ladies and gentlemen, we have a special presentation to mark the auspicious occasion of this our 'one hundredth' event. Each and every year, this proud village has superbly adorned itself with the most beautiful and imaginative gardens equal to anything witnessed in the length and breadth of this fair land of ours. Ouch!" She wittered on until feeling the force of Tarquini's foot on her ankle, realising the obvious hint to finish her speech and stopping her in full flow. "So, without further ado! Please be upstanding for Didsvale's Best Kept Village Centenary Celebration 'Lifetime Award' winner. Well, we have not just one, but two distinguished winners, who I'm sure will be equally overjoyed to receive this award donated by Lord Didsvale... The Honeysuckle sisters!" Dotty barked out. The loudest round of applause of the evening rang out from the collective appreciation of every attendee. Hattie and Hanna Honeysuckle were Didsvale's longest living residents. Both in their nineties, they were the much-respected stalwarts of the village. It was their efforts over many years to promote and organise the event and selfishly exclude themselves from competition entry. Dotty had deliberately placed the Honeysuckle sisters nearest her table so as to get this particular part of the ceremony over as quickly as possible, considering the time it would take for them to amble to the presentation table. Meanwhile, Tarquini was reaching down and placed a hand on one of the trophy's handles in preparation for the presentation. As he did so, his vintage, diamond encrusted, gold Swiss watch appeared from underneath his coat sleeve with its hands displaying the time of seven thirty. He reached forward with his other exposed hand shaped to receive handshakes from the doddering approaching sisters. Without any further ado and with a single action, he pushed the velvet cloth away from the trophy and lifted it up in full vision for all to admire, who then gasped in awe as one at the impressive, magnificent, gleaming, solid silver trophy award. With a desperate lurch forward, which almost forced the Honeysuckle sisters backwards, Tarquini thrust the trophy into their combined brittle bodies. With one eye on his watch's second hand now confirming the time, he ensured that the trophy stayed within his grasp. The Honeysuckle sisters placed a hand each on one handle of the trophy while Tarquini held his hand firmly onto the other. With the strongest determination, the sisters began to pull the trophy towards them, while Scumbali, with equal determination, tugged in the opposite direction, unwilling to release the other trophy handle for his own sinister motive. It was a motive now about to shock everyone at the garden party to the very core.

# Chapter 13
## The Countdown Continues

A few minutes prior, back at the engine shed, Toby had been calmly interpreting the SMEW operator's manual to upload Scumbali's instructions as Olive and Libby looked on. He checked the time on his watch, which showed seven twenty-five exactly. "Mmmm. I see!" he mused, staring intently but calmly as he turned the final page. "We're almost out of magicmunchymulch juice as it shows on the gauge, but here goes. We need you back quickly, Ahab, with more magicmunchymulch, and as soon as you possibly can!" He started to tap numerous keys simultaneously, moved his feet to depress the foot pedals and then, with a final flourish, pulled out an organ stop displaying the specific illustration he needed to select, which then sprang back again into its original position. "That should do it!" he announced, leaning back in nodding self-approval. The row of Squawkerlingo pipes, which were silent, suddenly burst into life with the most complex, nonsensical arrangement of musical notes you could imagine, before descending back from their crescendo into silence after a few seconds. "I think that must mean 'affirmative'!" he confidently confirmed to the others. He gave another check of his digital watch as the quartz numerals changed from 19.29.57 to 19.29.58 to 19.29.59 and then 19.30.00! "We have lift off!" he declared with eyes wide open, seeking a response from the SMEW machine.

"OK. Now what?" Libby queried. Just as those words left her mouth, she felt a sudden light shudder coming from within the study. Olive clung onto her mother, having felt the same experience, who in turn steadied the two of them by grabbing the back of Toby's shoulder.

Toby, who had been glaring at SMEW'S sophisticated console, replied in fascination, "Now this!" he replies as the whole study, with the Adamsons looking around with amazed expressions, felt themselves starting to revolve around with the study.

"We're moving!" Olive cried out. After no more than a few seconds the room stopped revolving, at which point Libby and Olive re-steadied themselves as the room came to an abrupt halt by clicking into position, forcing them off balance for a second.

"Look! See what's happened," said Toby in amazement, grabbing their attention and indicating to them where the compass's needle was now pointing to on the console. "The turntable and the Flying Cootsman have responded to my coordinate and instruction inputs by moving us all into the S.S.W.R. position. We started at due north and now we're now pointing towards south by south-west recurring! All I can say is 'mission accomplished' and over to Scumball's dirty deeds!" Libby looked at Toby in trepidation at what they had been ordered to put into action in exchange for Captain Ahab's innocence.

# Chapter 14
## The Garden Party is Rudely Interrupted

Meanwhile, back at the garden party, the toing and froing battle between Tarquini and the award-winning Honeysuckle sisters continued as they both hung on desperately to their side of the covetous 'Life Time Award' trophy. As the battle commenced, Tarquini with his fake accent again said, "Well done and congratulations to these amazing sisters and worthy winners of my special trophy." He released his grip on the trophy handle causing the sisters to fall backwards in surprise, complete with trophy, onto the neatly mown soft turf, both with legs akimbo. Tarquini focused onto his watch as it moved a few seconds past the seven thirty p.m. deadline. His concentration was no longer focused on the momentarily crestfallen recipients, but to the laurel bushes surrounding the garden parameter that were now becoming eerily silhouetted against the fading evening sky beyond. It was then that two jackdaws fluttered into the garden to land and sit statue-like on top of one of the nearest bushes. They were quickly followed by several more pairs that swooped and fluttered in and around the guests from above. Without anyone noticing, Tarquini held out his hand offering his glinting, diamond encrusted, gold wristwatch for easier access to the aerial interlopers. Dotty, similarly unnoticed, unclipped her diamond earrings, holding them in one hand before also revealing them to the approaching birds. Both actions worked perfectly and immediately caught the greedy eyes of one particular pair of jackdaws, who descended rapidly to claw Tarquini's treasured gold wristwatch away from his hand and quickly fly up and away to make their escape over the village hall roof. "Help!" he cried out dramatically, aiming to gain the attention of as many witnesses as possible. "Look! Those crow things have robbed my watch and Miss D'eath's earrings!" During the course of the next few seconds, the jackdaws worked in pairs, detecting and grabbing other gleaming rich pickings that caught their eyes, in accordance with the instructions Tarquini had left Toby with to carry out back at the engine shed. Glimmering tie pins, earrings, watches, brooches, necklaces, chains, rings and other items of value and sentiment were ripped away from their owners by the merciless and brainwashed jackdaws. The resulting scene was one of panic, pandemonium and devastation as each guest tried unsuccessfully to fend off the SMEW-programmed squadron of assailants. After the initial assault, the first pair of jackdaws to arrive had now left their perches during the height of the heist and swooped down towards the Honeysuckle sisters, still struggling to regain their footing after their mishap but then unceremoniously reintroduced to the soft garden turf by the swooping birds. In one joint 'swoosh', the two jackdaws grabbed a handle of the shiny trophy each before ascending effortlessly with it up and over the eaves of the village hall, then beyond the silhouetted trees towards Didsvale Park. The Didsvale Dynamo's very own Nellie Buchanan's pencil couldn't write fast enough to describe the unfolding event.

Unfortunately, her camera had also become a casualty of the previous melee and had broken into pieces by the stampede of panicking feet. As the hubbub died down, Tarquini cried out once again to the shocked and dazed guests, pointing at the last two assailants as they flew away firmly gripping their bounty. Tarquini alerted it to more witnesses, shouting, "The trophy. The trophy! Our special solid silver, our once in a lifetime, priceless solid silver trophy has also been stolen from our lovely Honeysuckle Sisters by mora ova those demon birds! It looks like they're heading for the park!" With the guests distracted by the concern for each other's welfare, Tarquini bent down under the table to find a dishevelled and cowering Dotty, and said to her, "Smooth as clockwork, Dotty. I've now got some unfinished business with those interfering Adamsons back at the engine shed. Here's the final part of the plan again." Dotty nodded positively as she remembered the plan; despite her obvious mesmerised and confused expression, Tarquini continued unabated, "Once I'm there, I'll say I retrieved all the stolen articles except the trophy and my vintage watch by fighting off those winged assassins, and return the articles back right here to their rightful owners tonight. It'll be another pip on the shoulder of Tarquini Scumbali, saviour of Didsvale Village. We'll keep the expensive trophy and my two hundred-thousand-pound Swiss watch for my finger-licking insurance claim, as planned. I have arranged a deal for a friend to melt the trophy down and forward my watch to an awaiting buyer who will give us a tidy lucrative profit. You must excuse yourself, Dotty, then make your way back to the manor and put the drones on standby just as I showed you, in case the smarty pants Adamsons try anything clever. If they do cause any trouble, I'm depending on you to ensure the drones guide me back to the manor safely. I'm not expecting them to have the tiniest intellect to outsmart me so we can soon start making plans for our money-spinning, spinning wind turbine and for the next Lady Didsvale's future!" He gently kissed the back of her hand as she swooned wide-eyed at him before he rapidly exited through the patio doors and on his way to the engine shed, leaving the garden party debacle behind him. From inside the hall, his voice could be heard by the distraught villagers in the garden, shouting. "Stopa thieves. You won't a getaway with this!"

A lone voice from somewhere in the scattered, staggering crowd shouted back in response, "Be careful, Lord Didsvale! Don't be a hero!" at which point Dotty reappeared from underneath the table, looking in the direction of where Tarquini's voice had come from, adding her own melodramatic sentiment for the crowd by screaming at the top of her voice, "Yes, Lord Didsvale! You are already Didsvale's hero. You don't need to convince us any more!"

# Chapter 15
## Back at the Engine Shed

Toby, Libby and Olive had been waiting nervously inside Peregrine's study for Tarquini's jackdaw instructions to be fully carried out. Toby turned away from the SMEW's console to confront the others. "Well, that's that, and just in the nick of time," he said with relief as he pointed to the fading magicmunchymulch gauge light. "That indicates it's now as good as empty, I'm afraid. We wouldn't have been able to keep Peregrine's work going in any case without more juice. Anyway, let's concentrate on the here and now. We need to keep our cool but it looks as though Scumbali has got us all over the proverbial barrel. It looks as though the family Adamsons are on their way out of Didsvale Village, barring a miracle. However, let's imagine that the professor's love of birds is like our family motto…!" at which point Toby invited them all to huddle together to say in unison:

*"Through all weathers the Adamsons will try, then onwards and upwards they to fly!"* Once they had finished reciting the motto, they opened the soundproof hatch and resurfaced onto the turntable.

As they did so, Toby stroked the side of the Flying Cootsman apologetically, saying, "Sorry SMEW! It wasn't your fault that you were tricked!" They waited anxiously by the locked engine shed doors with their heads pressed firmly against them, listening for the flapping wings of the returning jackdaws outside and from above the engine-shed roof. Before long, they heard the steady jangling noises as the returning jackdaws released their stolen hoard from on high, and for it to bounce and then settle into the green mesh netting that Libby had stretched over the discarded coalbunker earlier. There was one last thud as the last pair of jackdaws arrived with Tarquini's silver trophy and dropped it safely into the soft cushion of the same netting.

"That sounds like the evil mission has been accomplished!" said Libby resignedly.

"Indeed!" Toby agreed. "I wonder what happens next?"

No sooner had he got the words out of his mouth than he could hear running footsteps approaching the door before coming to a sudden halt. Next came a bout of heavy intakes of breathing and wheezing before the noise of a key began jangling in the keyhole. The Adamsons jumped back to safety from the door as it burst open to reveal the menacing figure of the returning Tarquini Scumbali, sweating from head to foot! "Well done, my friends! I knew you wouldn't let me down," he announced with his normal sarcasm. The green netting, which had acted as the capture trampoline for the stolen goods, was now draped over one shoulder with the contents being grasped with a single hand in front. Grasped firmly in the other hand was the solid silver trophy. Indicating at the green netting and its valuable content with a swift nod of his head, he said, "You must excuse me! I must return these to their rightful owners this evening and once again be declared as Didsvale's superhero by our wonderfully appreciative villagers. My modesty should prevent me from taking the acclaim but I'm afraid I'll have to let it take advantage of my better nature!" he added with such arrogance. "Anyway, there is one last favour I need to ask, which escaped my mind earlier. You! Mr Nosey Parker! Write down these new instructions and coordinates."

Toby looked at him disdainfully as he took another small piece of paper from Scumbali's hand and said, "I'm sorry we can't do this. It's impossible! We're completely out of…"

"Out of what?" Tarquini asked suspiciously.

Suddenly, Toby recomposed himself from his initial desperate response by almost confessing that they were out of magicmunchymulch and corrected himself with some quick thinking. "…We're completely out of… paper…! No, it's OK, I've found some. OK, what is it you want us to do for you next?" he asked while looking sideways at Libby with a relieved look, which went unnoticed by Tarquini.

"What you will do for me next is to instruct those clever jackdaws again to collect and deliver this trophy and this watch to these coordinates, seeing as they did such a good job to get them this far…" He hesitated briefly before adding menacingly… "and from your very own incriminating instructions!" He knew precisely what predicament he'd put the Adamsons in by lying to them. He placed his retrieved Swiss watch into the trophy and placed it carefully on the floor. "My associate will confirm to me that this has been done immediately after its safe delivery in a few hours, as I have calculated. Alas, I must take leave of you all again to return these articles back safely to the village hall and their worried owners. And just so I know you can't get up to any mischief, I need to ensure you stay here until I get back!" He snatched his written instructions back off Toby, turned on his heels and locked the engine shed doors together, with the Adamsons incarcerated once again inside as he departed.

Toby looked hopelessly at Libby. "What do we do now? We're out of magicmunchymulch juice fuel for SMEW. Tarquini's not going to be a happy bunny when that call doesn't come from his accomplice."

Libby turned to where Olive had been stood and said, "Don't worry, Olive, we'll sort things out. Olive? Olive?" Libby looked at the empty space where Olive had stood. She'd managed to climb onto the top of the Flying Cootsman so she could firstly reach, and then shin up, the dangling hose above it into the air vent. Libby and Toby heard a rattling noise from inside the air vent, which Olive had just managed to squeeze her slight frame through. Olive's heel could be seen disappearing from above the vent's tin cover flap as a little voice shouted from the roof outside.

"Don't worry! I'll soon sort things out! I'm just popping to the Bosun's Cabin to get Ahab back! Be back soon! Oh, and by the way. There's no sign of those drones you suspected, Mum, so you can't be overheard?" With that, she quickly disappeared entirely from view as the tin cover clattered back into place leaving her parents looking distinctly anxious. Incarcerated inside the locked engine shed they could hear her feet clambering safely down the sloping roof outside, before jumping the small drop onto the soft earth blow and scampering off to Bosun's Cabin.

Soaking with even more sweat, the self-appointed returning hero, Tarquini Scumbali, arrived back at the village hall to receive the full acclamation from the recovering garden party guests. Before coming into full view on the garden patio, he quickly took all the stolen personal effects from the green netting and placed them all, apart from his own watch, onto a serving tray before screwing up the mesh netting 'evidence' and prodding it deep into his trouser pocket. Adding to his heroic appearance he found an unused tomato ketchup sachet on the tray. Quickly tearing it open, he smeared the contents deliberately about his face and hands to give the fake impression of blooded injuries. With his make-up applied to full effect, he grabbed the serving tray by both side handles and stepped victoriously through the patio doors to confront his awaiting adoring fans. With a mass roar of cheering hysteria, the victims confronted his outstretched tray one by one to retrieve their valuables. At the end of the line were the Honeysuckle sisters, now fully restored to their most dignified, demure and well-presented appearances. As they approached, it was obvious that their special award trophy was missing from the tray of returned objects. Expecting their disappointment in advance, Tarquini looked at them both with the most hangdog expression he could muster on his uncompassionate face. "I'm really sorry, dear sisters. Your trophy was nowhere to be found. I grappled bravely with those dangerous birds and retrieved everything except your lovely trophy, which they flew away with into the distance. Rest assured, dear sisters, I shall have another one made for a you if it isn't found and returned." The Honeysuckle sisters looked appeased at Tarquini's convincing explanation and tottered away looking pretty pleased with Scumbali's compassionate compromise. Once again, in full view of the guests, he selected a pair of gold earrings from the tray before then addressing Dotty to cement the next stage of his outlandish plan. "Miss D'eath! I'm so delighted to reacquaint these beautiful and exquisite earrings with their beautiful and exquisite owner!"

Dotty blushed unashamedly before turning to the guests. "I can never thank you enough, Lord Didsvale. In fact, I think

I can say a heartfelt thank you on behalf of us all, for returning our treasured possessions in such a heroic way." At which juncture, the whole garden erupted into further clapping and cheering.

"I'm afraid I must leave you again to check that nothing has been stolen from Didsvale Manor, heaven forbid!" Tarquini's brief apology was swiftly followed by his second swift exit.

Dotty spoke up. "And I must drive home to check that no other jewellery has been taken from my home. I'm sure I left a bedroom window open. Thank you all once again for your patience. Rest assured, I shall get to the bottom of this unwarranted attack by these uncontrollable, horrid pests and bring our village back to its normal peaceful existence! Perhaps they are simply jealous that our new turbines plans have disrupted their scavenging lifestyles!" To a chorus of agreeing plaudits, Dotty strode urgently across the lawn to the patio door and made her own exit. Once outside, she ran to her sports car and then started it, before skidding off the car park gravel and speeding off towards Didsvale Manor. It was only a few minutes later that she hurtled past Kingfisher Cottage and rattled across the cattle grid and onto the long sweeping drive up to the manor house. Parking her car immediately by the front door, she got out and bounded up the steps and entered with the spare key that Scumbali had given her. After racing up the stairs, she barged into his study and reacquainted herself with his computer and bank of monitors. Tapping away vigorously into the keypad, she sat back, watching one monitor in particular crackle into life. Slowly, a gloomy image appeared from inside the huge truck parked outside, along with the sound of a loud humming noise. Then, as the truck's roof opened up and daylight shone into it, she could clearly see several small drones coming into view. They all began to hum softly and rise upwards. On the other six monitors, Dotty could see that they had all begun to fly out of the truck and then individually picked out the unmistakable shape of Tarquini's queen drone already on standby hovering above, waiting for their support. Leaning back on her chair with satisfaction, she began to speak to herself. "Well done, Dotty. Let's do this for my beloved Tarky Warky!"

Earlier, before Dotty had left the scene of complete disarray she had called the local policeman, Constable, Walker. She explained the situation and ordered him to get down to village hall urgently to take some eyewitness statements. Dotty realised that Nellie Buchanan would also be there to corroborate the story and provide ideal alibis for herself and Tarquini.

# Chapter 16
## Olive to the Rescue

Olive arrived hot foot back at Bosun's Cabin. She recited to herself what Ahab had said to find the hidden location of the door key, "... *'the first island to the west of Key West'*..." She then looked under the first lump of white rockery featuring the letter 'K' and heaved it over to find a large brown, rusting key underneath. Picking it up, she ran to the door, unlocked it and entered. After some clattering from inside the cabin, the front wheel of Peregrine's old bike emerged from the front door. Then, Olive's small outstretched hands appeared, grasping the bike's front handlebar, guiding it outside. What came next was the comical sight of Olive, shrouded in Peregrine's old large school gown with his school cap balanced back to front on her tiny head. She gathered up the excess gown and placed it in the attached basket and fondly announced, "Wherever your trusty bike goes, Professor Peregrine Greylag, so does your cap and gown!" Bouncing it down a couple of wooden steps in front of the cabin, she guided the bike until it was standing at ground level. Standing on the first step to give her body extra height, she swung one leg over the bike's crossbar and placed the other firmly onto the first step to steady her body with. With one foot on the raised pedal and the other on the second pedal, she then leant her upper body against the post for extra balance well in good reach of the large shiny ship's bell. She was now in the ideal position for a speedy take-off by using only the pedals for balance because of the large bike's saddle being well out of reach for her tiny frame. Now, in the perfect position and with no more time to lose, she recited the words and began ringing the bell and made quacking noises…

"*Ring eight bells again while you quack like a duck and Argyll will return without any luck!*" …and so it went on until she gave the eighth 'ring' followed by the last 'quack'! She pushed away with as much force as she could against the post with both her feet placed on the pedals, launching herself and the bike forwards. Within a few metres, they had conquered gravity and with Olive standing upright using only the pedals for balance, she was now well and truly gathering pace for the ride back to the engine shed. Within minutes, she had made it to the River Babble Bridge crossing, where she was confronted by a huge tree-bending gust of wind blowing against her that forced her to stop it blowing away, she then witnessed the phenomenon of a huge single riptide wave, more than a metre high, racing upstream from the estuary and dying out to nothing just as it reached the river bridge. The gushing mini typhoon wind disappeared almost as soon as it had arrived and the bent trees returned to their original upright positions. Now safe to continue, Olive pushed away from the tree and pedalled on in her unorthodox style with full speed. In a flash, she suddenly realised what this peculiar scene meant by shouting out so gleefully it reverberated resoundingly through the surrounding trees as she propelled herself along. "Welcome back, Captain Ahab. Argyll has blown you back safely on the high tide with a little help from my ship's bell signal!"

# Chapter 17
# *Tarquini Returns*

Imprisoned back at the engine shed, Toby and Libby had tried to keep focussed and calm in Olive's absence and the impending re-arrival of Tarquini Scumbali, by examining the SMEW machine in precise detail. It wouldn't be long until they would have to confess to him that it would be impossible to carry out his instructions without a new batch of magicmunchymulch juice from Captain Ahab on his return from Pamona Atoll. The evil Tarquini still had the upper hand as nothing could be proved against his dirty deeds. Toby broke the silence created by their dual concentration to surmise. "So! When Tarquini gets back here, he'll assume that we've carried out his instruction to the word. When he finds out we haven't, well, who knows what that reprobate will do in addition to throwing us out of the village in shame and locking up poor old Captain Ahab. He's so in league with that corrupt Dotty D'eath that I bet she's covered his back about starting the wind turbine work before it was formally approved. We have no proof of any drones being used to cause Professor Peregrine's death. He's got us hook, line and sinker."

Reaching the engine shed, Olive dismounted Peregrine's bike before carefully propping it up against the wall. She left the cloak and cap behind, balanced on the bike's handlebars, then began to shin up the exterior drainpipe onto the roof. Toby and Olive's conversation suddenly stopped inside the engine shed as they heard a noise outside, and then the air-vent began to clatter as Olive's feet reappeared from above. After descending the water pipe and onto the Flying Cootsman, she slid down its boiler, landing safely on the turntable. Her relieved parents stood smiling at her. "I'm back!" Olive announced. Breathlessly, she began to tell them about her journey to Bosun's Cabin and the evidence she saw on the River Babble of Captain Ahab's return. No sooner had she finished her story than there was a loud rattling noise of the lock coming from the outside of the engine shed door. Realising that it may be Tarquini returning, Olive grabbed the trophy and its valuable contents and hid them out of view just to the side of the Flying Cootsman so he wouldn't be aware they failed his orders. On seeing her parents' desperate expressions to their dire plight, Olive scampered over to the turntable and disappeared underneath and back into Peregrine's study, closing the hatch cover behind her. She leapt into the chair attached to the SMEW machine, tapped in the letters S.M.E.W and began to concentrate on all the instruments as they reappeared. Up and down she scanned, mumbling to herself and addressing an imaginary Peregrine as she studied. "What have we missed, Professor Peregrine? Dad has read this manual from cover to cover umpteen times and he said not to touch these switches, as they weren't in the manual. What do these abbreviations mean? Keep calm, keep calm, Olive!" She continued to stare and stare at the letters on each switch trying to decipher what they stood for, and then suddenly her eyes lit up. "Oh Yes! Of course! So that's what they mean. Thank you, Peregrine. Let's try this one for starters." She leant forwards and flicked the switch with the abbreviations R.B.B.B.B. Almost immediately, a wooden section behind where the SMEW manual was placed, started to slide open. Olive watched patiently for a few seconds before leaning back into the chair looking aghast in complete surprise, as a broad smile of satisfaction spread across her face.

Suddenly, above her in the engine shed both of the large wooden doors flew open to reveal the indistinguishable shape of Tarquini Scumbali on his return, standing even more dishevelled than last time, dripping with sweat and slowly trying to control his exhausted breath. "H... H... H... H... hello my friends! Sorry to have kept you waiting. I'm so glad to see you've been so sensible as to stay put and decided to do what's best for all of us! So, I presume that you've carried out my second favour successfully with Professor Madcap's clever contraption?" he said offensively. Toby and Libby looked hopelessly at each other motionless in search of a response, knowing full well that they were unable to carry out his instructions. Libby whispered to Toby out of the corner of her mouth and stated, "Well, that's us now doomed and saying goodbye to Didsvale!"

While he was waiting for Toby and Libby to reply, Tarquini changed the subject. "Hey, where's that little brat of yours?" Suddenly, a little voice answered as Olive reappeared from beneath the Flying Cootsman. "I'm here, Lord Tarquini Didsvale! It's so nice to see you again," Olive shouted as she ran over to Scumbali and threw herself at his waist, wrapping her arms around him. "I was so frightened in here!" she sobbed in pretence. However, on her way over to greet Tarquini, she accidentally clipped the hidden silver trophy with her heel, making it roll into open view. As it stopped rolling, the Swiss watch then spilled out onto the floor catching Scumbali's attention as he stared with shock and surprise at the revelation. Taken aback and duped by her sudden act of favouritism towards him, he looked down and very sheepishly patted her head.

"You're OK now, my child. We're all safe now." He disengaged her arms awkwardly from him before pushing her back towards her parents, who both stood completely bemused by their daughter's uncharacteristic affection towards their evil nemesis. Tarquini diverted his attention back onto the trophy and watch, which he strode over towards to pick up then, glaring at Toby, asked accusingly, "And what may I ask are these doing here? You've betrayed me, haven't you?" No sooner had he got his words out than some steps could be heard moving outside the engine shed. Tarquini quickly stepped to one side of the door to hide out of view as the unmistakable giant outline form of Captain Ahab McCrab appeared in the doorway before stepping inside the engine shed. With one hand grasping the chord of his rucksack, he held a small glass phial clasped in the other hand and offered it to the Adamsons.

"There you are! More supplies of magicmunchymulch juice. Argyll did his job. I knew he wouldn't let us down. Well done, Olive, for remembering his rhyme!" Ahab bellowed out, unaware of the hiding Tarquini.

Toby, Libby and Olive smiled nervously at their returning friend, who looked puzzled by their obvious lack of enthusiasm. "I knew you would come back safely, Captain Ahab. It's so great to see you again!" said Libby while trying to indicate with a slight subtle nod of the head that Tarquini was hiding behind the door. As quick as a flash, Tarquini appeared and snatched the glass phial from Ahab's hand before he could react.

"OK Sailor Sam, you get over there with those grizzly Adamsons or I'll smash this magic potion stuff to smithereens. As for you, Crabbie McCrab, I've got enough evidence on you for the theft of my antique carriage clock for them to put you away for a very, very long time!"

"So, it was you who planted it in my boat? You rascal and a half!" Ahab replied angrily to Tarquini as he went to lamp him one with his fist.

Tarquini reeled backwards, making a threatening action to smash the precious glass phial. "Steady on, Sailor Sam. One more quick, clever move like that and whatever liquid there is in here will be a gonner, I promise. Just like you will be quite soon!"

"Promise? You don't know the meaning of the word. Like the promise you made to me to extend my rent on Kingfisher Cottage?" retorted Captain Ahab.

"Let's just say it was a business transaction and not exactly my fault you weren't intellectually well up in that area. Anyway, these lovely Adamson people have enjoyed your cottage since. You wouldn't want to offend them now, would you? Well, that's enough small talk for now. I must be getting on with my plans to bring new prosperity to the villagers of Didsvale. You can all then scarper off out of my way to a land far, far away!" Tarquini scowled.

Suddenly, Olive, who had been cowering behind Toby and Olive, bravely edged forward towards Tarquini, ignoring Libby's desperate plea. "No Olive! What are you doing? He's mad!"

Tarquini noticed Olive's approach and shouted out, "And

163

where do you think you're going, small fry? Just stay right there!"

Olive stood fully upright with her shoulders back and spoke calmly and confidently to Tarquini. "Dear Mr Scumbali, before you carry out your threats to my mum and dad and our dear friend, Captain Ahab, there are just a few things that I think you should know before we all part our ways and end our wonderful friendship with you!"

Tarquini looked down at her and replied with a bemused look, "What on earth are you talking about, sprat?"

"Well, they say it takes a sprat to catch a mackerel and you're nothing but a fishy character, Mr Scumball! Here's one thing I'm talking about," Olive retorted to him and then turned to address the others. "What Lord Fake Didsvale here hadn't taken into account was how ingenious our wonderful Professor Peregrine Greylag was by setting up CCTV cameras in his various bat boxes placed strategically around the park and nature reserve. Dad! Those initials we noticed on the SMEW console switches are all abbreviations for his bat boxes: R.B.B.B.B., which stands for River Babble Bridge Bat Box; and N.R.B.B., which stands for Nature Reserve Bat Box. I've just seen replays of a panicking Peregrine being chased by your drones from your manor house and across the nature reserve, before eventually forcing him off his bike and into the mighty oak tree where he met his end! Not only that, but these cameras also show one of your dastardly drones placing a carriage clock into the hold of the Pretty Pol just before Ahab set sail for Pamona Atoll.

Toby couldn't help contain his excitement at Olive's revelation. "Yes! Result! Great work, Inspector Olive!" He then glared threateningly at Tarquini.

Olive smiled proudly at her parents before turning back to glare at Tarquini, standing in complete shock with eyes and mouth wide open while trying to take in her surprising revelation. She continued. "Not only that!" She then reached into the back pocket of her dungarees and pulled out pieces of paper. Without turning around, handed them blindly backwards to her parents. "We also have this incriminating evidence against you, Mr Scumball!"

Libby reached out and grabbed the pieces of paper Olive was holding out. Toby looked on as Libby unfolded the next item of potential evidence and found herself looking at the two sets of instructions written in Tarquini's very own incriminating handwriting. Raising her head from the paper notes, after realising what Olive had done, she said, "So, that's what those little melodramas of yours were about when you hugged this scoundrel. I thought it was a bit out of character!"

Olive replied. "All of that rehearsing for one of Fagin's pickpockets in the school play came to good use after all!" she explained with a beaming smile.

"Oh. You're such a brave cookie. Well done. You know what this means. It means we now have some useful evidence," Libby concluded.

Olive stared at Tarquini with the most fearsome expression she could make and said, "So, I put it to you, Lord Fake Didsvale of Nowhere, that this jury finds you well and truly guilty. I can confirm that this little sprat has caught this large smelly mackerel in her net, where he'll be grilled and eaten up by the law!"

By this time, Tarquini's eyes were gazing straight ahead and fixed in full shock. His hands shook uncontrollably as the realisation of Olive's extra indisputable evidence slowly dawned upon him.

With nothing to lose, Ahab strode forwards to stand face-to-face with Tarquini. Slowly pulling the rucksack from off his shoulder he said, "And how about a feel of your precious carriage clock with the compliments of Sailor Sam!" He released the rucksack chord with its heavy clock inside from his grip, which was followed by an almighty scream of pain from Tarquini as it landed squarely on his foot. In doing so, he released his grip on the glass phial of precious magicmunchymulch juice, forcing it to spin up through the air. As if in slow motion, they all looked on, watching it spinning and spiralling out of control. Then, as it descended back down towards the hard engine shed floor with impending shattering, Olive dived forward and caught it safely single-handedly.

Now, hopping about comically on one leg, Tarquini finally broke his silence to cry out. "Owwwwch! You've broken my toe you mighty lummox. You'll pay for this!" he said with a painful grimace.

"I've got nothing to pay you with, Tarquini, you scoundrel! I'm penniless remember? Which is why you threw me out of Kingfisher Cottage. So much for helping the villagers of Didsvale! What about the prosperity of this villager!" Ahab cried out, while pointing angrily to himself.

As the Adamsons and Ahab turned to each other to self-congratulate themselves, Tarquini chose this moment to escape while they were all distracted. Before anyone could react, he grabbed the silver trophy and his precious watch from the floor, which he then placed back onto his wrist before limping painfully towards the engine shed door. When he got outside, he quickly re-locked the door behind him snaring the others inside. He looked up to see his drones under Dotty

D'eath's command hovering above. Leaning against the door to take the weight off his injured foot, he shouted loudly through cupped hands somewhat breathlessly and in desperation towards his queen drone… *"GO FOR PLAN C, DOTTY—GET ME BACK SAFELY! HAVE CAR AND EMERGENCY CASES READY FOR OUR GETAWAY—CALL HARRY ON THE NUMBER I GAVE YOU!"* He then mumbled to himself, "This is when I need you, the dearest, dippy, Dotty! I'm depending on you. Pllllease don't let me down! Plllllease!" Then, looking up again towards his drones, he shouted out, "Come on my beauties. Get me home. We can live to fight another day somewhere else!" He pushed himself away from the door and limped painfully and gingerly along the pathway towards Didsvale Manor to make his escape. Clasping the heavy trophy for all that it was worth, he cried out in pain with each step as he went, "Ooh, ooh! Aaah! Owch, Owch, Owch… I hate those Adamsons!"

# Chapter 18
## The Chase to River Babble Bridge

Back inside the engine shed, the prisoners had gathered together. "We can't let him get away with this!" shouted Toby angrily.

OK. Stand well back, I'm coming through," ordered Ahab as he ran past them towards the locked door, shoulder first. As he barged into the door with all the Herculean force he possessed, the solid oak doors swayed back and forth but the lock held firm despite his strenuous effort, forcing him to repel backwards into the engine shed. Rubbing his shoulder in defeat he turned to the others. "It's not budging. If there's one thing I know about Peregrine, it's when he made something, he made it well!" he confessed. "OK, we must all stick together and use our noggins to get us all out of here and stop that rascal escaping somehow. Where's young Olive gone to now?" he queried. While Toby and Libby were watching Ahab's brave, unsuccessful efforts to break through the locked door, Olive had run sharply over to the turntable and descended back into the underground study without anyone noticing. Slowly, she brought her anxious, panting breath under control before sitting with a look of full concentration and determination at the controls of the SMEW machine, with the tiny glass phial of magicmunchymulch juice firmly grasped in her hand. With the greatest of care, she unscrewed its lid and reached up to the small funnel and delicately began to pour the juice into it saying, "I guess this goes in here!" With the glass phial now entirely empty, she sat back into the seat awaiting some kind of response. Then, after a few seconds, a weird brown and green glow appeared from within the console's small glass window. Olive's eyes opened to their full extent, fascinated by the reaction. Then something strange happened. One of the notelets suddenly became unstuck and fluttered downwards before resting on Olive's hand. Then, gazing at the sticky notelet with the wording '*S. D. M.—R & D—must only be used in an emergency for happy memory assistance*' written on it, she took a quick intake of breath in surprise, then began to whisper to the absent professor. "Thanks Professor Peregrine. Can this sticker help us somehow? That horrible Tarquini Scumbali was nasty to you and we know what happened. We've followed all of your clues so far and because this is an emergency and we could sure do with a Silver Dream Machine happy memory emergency right now! This is our last chance, Peregrine, and about as an emergency as emergencies get! I hope you don't mind me trying it out! So, here goes." Then, without further hesitation, she reached into her top dungaree zip pocket and carefully brought out the postcard that she'd earlier stored away for safekeeping. Reaching forward, she carefully presented it to the slot on SMEW'S facia and gently pushed it in until it completely disappeared. She then reached further up to turn the compass dial to the S.S.W.R. direction before closing her eyes and crossing her fingers in anticipation. Then, unbeknown to Olive, a mysterious thing was coincidentally happening as she watched the souvenir postcard gradually disappear into the Silver Dream Machine slot! Peregrine's cap and gown, which were earlier resting on his bike outside the engine shed where Olive had left them, completely evaporated into thin air leaving the bike still balanced against the engine shed wall. In addition to this weird happening, the central turntable supporting the Flying Cootsman slowly readjusted itself to the South by South-West Recurring direction to align with the exit track leading to the engine shed doors. Underground in the study, where Olive still sat with her eyes closed and fingers crossed, she felt a sudden jolt from above. On opening her eyes, Olive could see that the study ceiling began to open downwards and the SMEW's pipe organ housing started to fold away. She quickly pushed her chair backwards and safely away from the SMEW consoles. In one continuous movement, the entire machine folded back into itself and started to rise upwards through the reopened ceiling hatch and back into the Flying Cootsman's boiler, from where it had originally descended, whirring as it went along the attached metal pulleys and small pieces of railway track. Olive gazed through the ceiling hatch to see the track settle into its original position immediately underneath the steam engine above, just as the ceiling door hatch slowly closed. She heard an almighty roar and hiss from the Flying Cootsman above as she sprung into life with steam beginning to burst out of every piston. With the door now inches from being fully closed, a few last wisps of steam managed to enter the study just as it softly clicked to. Without hesitation, Olive scampered up the steps and onto the turntable before jumping onto the steam engine's cab, and onto its seat. With steam swirling around her, she began to whisper, "So, I've managed to get this far,

Peregrine, what next?" As she peered through the steam, she became aware of another figure beside her and began to ask, "Mum? Dad? Captain Ahab? Is that you?"

The steam started to clear around her for a split second as she took a sharp, startled intake of breath at the figure sat revealed beside her. "No, it's none of them, Olive. It's me, Professor Peregrine Greylag! I can't tell you how chuffed I am. Chuffed! Get it? I'm so chuffed that you and your family managed to crack the SMEW's code and finally bring my special Flying Cootsman to life again. You've also experimented with my Silver Dream Machine, I see, and posted the postcard I left for you all to find. How wonderful. I'm also chuffed to bits that you and your parents all used my keys to good effect after cleverly resolving the riddles, as I knew you would of course! As you could see, that postcard picture is one of my fondest memories of the Flying Cootsman. When the Silver Dream Machine connected with the global polar magnetic brainwave deep blue vortex on Pamona Atoll, it summoned me with this happy memory back to this very happy place! And so here I am!" he explained, then asked, "Tell me, Olive. What type of emergency do you need that required this action and brought me back to share my temporary 'happy memory' reality with you?"

Olive was still recovering from the shock of finding the youthful Peregrine sitting next to her complete with his cap and gown, but eventually found her voice again and responded. "You look just like the professor Greylag in the postcard. You must help us. Please! Please! Professor Greylag?" she pleaded, and began to explain as fast as she could what Tarquini Scumbali had done to them all and was now escaping back to the manor house.

171

Peregrine hung on to every excitable word flying out of Olive's mouth before responding to the description of the Adamsons and Ahab's predicament with the evil Scumbali. "Now, I can see why it's such an emergency. That reprobate, Tarquini Scumbali, has a lot to answer for," he seethed. Fumbling underneath the panelling for something in front of where they sat, he turned to Olive saying, "There's the release button; just where I remembered it was." As he pushed the hidden button, the front facia board within the engine cab slowly began to rise upwards before folding backwards on itself at the top, revealing what was now familiar to Olive as the SMEW machine controls now firmly embodied back into the engine's boiler.

"It's just like the front panel on that concertina writing desk you left for me," Olive responded.

"Absolutely," Peregrine agreed, despite him being distracted by tapping furiously away at the keys, pulling the stops and pushing down on the foot pedals with both feet. After a few seconds, the pipes responded with a tumultuous whistling noise of confirmation. "I think that should do it, as I recall!" Peregrine announced confidently.

"May I ask another quick question, Professor Greylag?" Olive begged.

"Make it ultra-quick please, Olive. We need to be making tracks. Get it Olive. Tracks!" he quipped.

"Are the Younoseeme Squibrels real?" she mused.

"Of course. I couldn't have done this without them and now they have served their purpose, they have been returned home with Ahab as I promised! Why?" he replied.

"Oh nothing!" she added, raising a knowing smile to herself.

Without any further delay, Peregrine scanned around the Flying Cootsman's cab to re-acquaint himself with the controls as he spoke to Olive in the process. "Why, that good for nothing excuse of a human being, Tarquini Scumbali, and those drones of his are about to meet their match! You said he's limping his way back to Didsvale Manor? The only route for him to take will be alongside the railway track and across the River Babble Bridge through the nature reserve. Well, let's just see how he copes escaping from this little training session." At which point, Peregrine began pulling at several levers and turned a large wheel and pulled another handle lever outwards, which caused the Flying Cootsman to hiss even louder in response from her piston valves He turned to Olive and said, "OK. Put your trust in me, Olive. Pull that chord quickly and hang on!" She pulled the chord that he'd pointed to dangling by her side and the unmistakable sound of a coot's call resounded loudly around the engine shed, even drowning out the sound of the hissing steam valves. Peregrine then yanked another lever firmly downwards and kept it pressed down. Before she could ask any further questions, Olive found herself hanging on for dear life as the reinvigorated steam engine suddenly accelerated forward from its standing start, just like an Olympic sprinter being released out of the starting blocks, accelerated towards the closed engine shed doors.

Toby, Libby and Captain Ahab were anxiously chattering amongst themselves to find a solution to the situation and were completely oblivious to Olive's independent actions in Peregrine's underground study. Before they could move from their positions, they found themselves being enveloped in the clouds of steam emitting from the Flying Cootsman and unable to move in any direction. From inside the steam came the deafening noise of a train's whistle forcing them to cover their ears for protection. Suddenly, the steam was rapidly blown away by the force of the Flying Cootsman bursting forwards as her front name-plaque came prominently into view. The three alarmed figures jumped to one side as the Flying Cootsman flew past them, demolishing the engine shed's locked doors into pieces as she burst through them with ease. As she passed by, with steam still swirling around the engine's cab, they could hear Olive shouting at the top of her voice, "Captain Ahab! Summon Argyll again with the bells as fast as you can."

As the engine sped past him, Ahab was just about able to catch a glimpse through a gap in the thick enveloping steam of Olive sitting in the engine's cab with Peregrine next to her at the controls. Taking his cap off to scratch his head vigorously in wonderment, he whispered to himself, "Well, I'll be blown! It's the professor himself coming to the rescue!"

Toby and Libby had missed this because they were still standing defensively, eyes closed with both hands on their ears. However, Libby managed to catch Ahab saying something and asked, "What did you say, Ahab?" But before she received any reply, Ahab had swung his heavily laden rucksack effortlessly over one shoulder and then dashed through the demolished engine shed doorway in response to Olive's instruction. Running frantically around the back of the engine shed, he found Peregrine's bike. In one complete motion, he grabbed its handlebars and with a solitary foot on one pedal and his hand gripping the handle bar he swung his huge body over the bike frame to land with a hefty bump onto the saddle. Then, placing the other foot on the other pedal pushed away and raced off as fast as he could towards Bosun's

Cabin. Toby and Libby stood bewildered without a clue what to do in the circumstances. Suddenly, Toby noticed that the Flying Cootsman had departed with such force she had blown the surrounding undergrowth outside the engine shed completely flat, revealing an old rusting object. "Look over there, Libby; an old pump trolley on a hidden piece of track!"

"What on earth is that?" she queried.

"You know," he replied. "You remember in those old films when those flat-shaped trolleys propelled along the train track by two passengers pumping furiously up and down on those seesaw handles to keep it moving? Well, that's what it is, a pump trolley!

"Can I guess what you're thinking now?" asked Libby.

"I think you already know the answer to that one!" Toby responded. Then, without any further hesitation, the two of them jumped onto the pump cart and pushed down on a handle each for all they were worth. Slowly but surely, the pump trolley moved forward and quickly gained pace from their joint efforts and away from the engine shed.

# Chapter 19
## Fending Off the Drones

From Tarquini's study back at Didsvale Manor, Dotty stood anxiously at the drone controls being able to hear and see the preceding events unfold through Tarquini's queen drone sensors. She was operating this, together with the other drones, as best she could despite her obvious inexperience. Barely unable to believe her eyes, she had seen the Flying Cootsman and its passengers burst though the locked engine shed doors in the direction of her hapless hero. "I'll get you back safely, my darling. You can always trust in me, Tarky Warky!" she said to herself as she nervously and furiously tapped away at the controls. After seeing the events unfold in the engine shed onwards, she moved the queen drone and the rest of the lesser drones towards the limping Tarquini. She could clearly see through the queen drone's camera that he was now sitting on a log resting his injured foot. "Come on, Dotty, you can do this. You can save poor Tarky!" she blurted to herself while guiding the queen drone to hover immediately above the sitting figure below. Then, with a few dextrous movements of her fingers, released a large grabbing arm from the drone's underbelly. With the help of its remote camera, she delicately lowered the arm to a point just above and behind the unsuspecting Tarquini. Then, like an amusement arcade grabber about to capture a cuddly toy, the arm hooked onto his braces at the rear. Having regained his breath and about to limp off again, he found his efforts to move forward thwarted by an opposite force coming from behind. He gasped with fear and dread as his feet lifted off the ground with the trophy firmly in his grip, before being whisked towards the tree canopy above. With his feet kicking hopelessly in all directions, he looked above to see himself attached to the rescuing queen drone and realised what was happening.

"Well done, Dotty, I knew you could do it!"

With Tarquini's queen drone now preoccupied with transporting its suspended, flying passenger to safety, the six smaller support drones held back to defend them against the approaching Flying Cootsman, with Peregrine and Olive, gaining ground in pursuit. Peregrine turned to Olive and said, "It looks as though we have a challenge on our hands, Olive!" as the drones closed in, buzzing across and above from all angles, attempting to dislodge them from their seats.

"Leave it to me, Peregrine. Put your trust in me this time!" Olive said turning sideways and giving a confident wink to the engine driver. Without hesitation, she unzipped the top pocket of her dungarees and brought out the 'Y'-shaped piece of oak branch and one of the acorns that she had kept from the previous day. She then placed one of the acorns into the spare hairband that she kept in the same pocket and by using it as a catapult, took aim. As the first drone swept by she released her ammunition in its direction. With deadly accuracy, it hit the drone directly on its red remote direction sensor. "Bull's eye!" she cried out as it spiralled wildly out of control as a result.

"Great shot, Olive," Peregrine commentated.

Over at Tarquini's study, Dotty D'eath looked at the

screen and noticed the sudden interference on the drone screen. Desperately banging the keyboard, she shouted with concern. "What's happened there?" It was only when she looked at the other monitors that she noticed that one of the drones wasn't responding. "Oh well. Never mind, Dotty. One down, five more left! I'll take care of that blasted train and its passengers," she said to herself encouragingly.

Speeding along in the cab of the Flying Cootsman, Olive continued her conversation with Peregrine. "Well, that's one down and five to go!" she added, and then picked off the other five with similar accuracy within minutes as they flew within striking distance of her deadly acorn catapult. "Sttttrrrrrike number six," she screamed out as the last drone hurtled out of control before crashing to the ground and shattering into pieces.

By this point, Dotty was crumbling apart as she witnessed another acorn approaching the last drone with deadly accuracy. She held her breath as Olive's acorn grew larger and larger on the monitor before it hit its target and left another drone downed and another screen crackling in defeat. The only monitor now left working efficiently now showing the queen drone making its way back to Didsvale Manor, although having become much slower due to the heavy weight of Tarquini and his trophy swinging uncontrollably from side-to-side underneath. "Come on, Dotty. All is not lost. Keep it together!" she said, aiming to comfort herself over the preceding debacle and the destruction of Tarquini's cherished drones by Olive's acorn onslaught.

On board the Flying Cootsman, Peregrine and Olive could clearly make out Tarquini's flailing body in the near distance, suspended beneath the queen drone like a puppet being operated by a drunken puppeteer. They could see the drone had slowed down under Tarquini's weight and the speeding Flying Cootsman was fast gaining ground. Across River Babble Bridge they all went and deep into the nature reserve where Tarquini had shrouded the tree canopy with his controversial netting.

Dotty D'eath was still struggling with the queen drone's controls and was attempting to guide it and Tarquini back to safety to make their escape. However, with the Flying Cootsman closing in so fast and distracted by this, she accidentally guided him past Didsvale Manor and back towards the nature reserve forest. She found herself watching Tarquini waving frantically trying to attract her attention suspended beneath. Dotty could just about hear his voice blasting out towards her through the thick window glass panel. "What on earth are you doing, Dotty? Get me down, you mad woman!" His cry of help was to no avail though as she fiddled once again with the controls, trying to keep him ahead of the merciless Flying Cootsman and her vengeful occupants, who were also looping back towards the nature reserve, hot on Tarquin's flying heels. Dotty certainly hadn't taken this into account and wept uncontrollably at her hero's predicament.

# Chapter 20
## Ahab Beckons Argyll

With all the commotion happening away in the distance, Ahab arrived at Bosun's Cabin on Peregrine's bike. Without bothering to dismount it, he grasped at the bell's dangling rope and hung onto it to steady himself with one foot placed firmly on the ground. In the next seamless motion, he began to recite as he gave the bell's rope a quick tug, *"'As the last of eight bells ends its ring, mighty Argyll will take to wing. He'll billow your sails and give you speed, to Pamona Atoll for the juice we need'."* On completion of the instruction to Argyll, he pushed away again on Peregrine's bike and sprinted back in the direction of the old ferry landing, saying to himself the following words as he left, "Let's hope this works, Ahab! We've nothing to lose."

Toby and Libby were now moving along on the pump trolley at a fair pace. "We just need to change that point lever up ahead with something without losing speed?" Toby suggested.

"I've got an idea. Keep pumping your handle as fast as you can please, Toby," Libby suggested as she began to remove Peregrine's telescope from around her neck, saying apologetically, "I'm sorry, Peregrine, but I think you'll understand why I'm doing this." She waited until the pump trolley drew level with the points lever by the track before swinging Peregrine's telescope and connecting with it full on. The lever sprang forwards as a result, allowing the point mechanism to allow the pump trolley to carry on without being derailed. Looking at the damaged end of the telescope caused by the impact, Libby said, "Whoops! I'll have it fixed as soon as I can, Peregrine. I promise!" She then placed the telescope back around her neck and grabbed both sides of the pump trolley for stability as Toby pushed furiously up and down on the handle in an attempt to stay in touch with the Flying Cootsman up ahead. As they rattled along, Libby bravely balanced herself enough to extend the telescope to its full length and looked through it to try and make out what was going on in the distance. Unfortunately, the impact had loosened the end of the telescope. "Damn it!" she exclaimed to herself. "I'm really sorry, Peregrine. I'll have it repaired once we're out of the woods, literally! But it still works though."

"What... was... that?" Toby attempted to ask Libby to repeat herself, but quickly gave up asking due to his strenuous exertions in keeping the pump trolley gliding along the track towards River Babble Bridge and across into Didsvale Manor estate. On the pair went in pursuit of the Flying Cootsman, which in turn was in pursuit of Tarquini Scumbali hanging onto the queen drone, who was also now in desperate pursuit of... A quick escape!

The pump trolley rolled along at an increasingly fast pace, responding to Toby's exertions on the pump handle. Libby was focussing the damaged telescope up ahead out of one eye when she suddenly noticed something coming up into view to one side out of the corner of her other semi-closed eye. It was the front wheel and handlebars of Peregrine's bike with Ahab on board that had caught up with them. Ahab's mighty hands could be seen gripping the handlebars, and as the bike gradually began to overtake them, his arms and then his full profile appeared huffing and puffing almost as loud as the Flying Cootsman, drawing level with them. He was taking in huge gasps of air as his legs applied full, constant power to the pedals. In doing so, he yelled across at the pump trolley with some extra energy, "I'll go on up ahead and see what's happening!"

Libby looked across and replied, "OK, Ahab, but be careful! Make sure Olive's all right, won't you!"

As the rear wheel of the bike overtook them, she heard Ahab's reply, "Don't worry about a thing. River Babble Bridge is just up ahead. We'll soon be across it and at the manor house!"

No sooner had Ahab's verbal guarantee been acknowledged by those on board the pump trolley, than its front wheels started to overtake Ahab's back wheel as his tiredness set in, causing the bike to slow down as Toby and Libby then overtook him in turn. The pump trolley sped along with its occupants, leaving Ahab to catch his second breath in the hope that he could make up ground with them later. Libby had the telescope pressed to her eye once again and reported back to Toby, now starting to wheeze heavily behind her. "All I can see are the wisps of trailing steam from the Flying Cootsman. They must be well ahead," she said as the pump trolley's sound changed from a continuous whirring noise into a deeper rattle as it trundled onwards across the River Babble's wooden bridge and into the nature reserve. Libby reported back again to Toby with an update, having seen through the telescope the distinct plume of engine steam continuing past

Didsvale Manor and along the loop line back towards the other side of the nature reserve. "They're coming back!" she announced with astonishment.

Toby replied as attentively as he could, despite his strenuous efforts. "What... do... you... mean," before screaming incredulously, "... coming... back!"

"Keep going, Toby! Maybe Scumball's tried to give them the slip and decided to hang about in the forest for a while," she concluded without realising the unintended pun! "I'm sure the mansion house is on a slight hill so we might be going downhill when we pass it!"

Not to be outdone, Captain Ahab regained his second wind and was now accelerating nicely. Across the River Babble Bridge he went, over the wooden planks next to the rail track, which shook and rattled his entire body by their unevenness. Undaunted by this teeth-rattling obstacle, he regained his balance and pressed onto the pedals even harder, determined to catch up with the others. The mighty reinvigorated frame of Captain Ahab overtook the pump trolley by the manor house, and then realising that he had swept by it, started to freewheel rapidly downhill towards the steam filled nature reserve forest into which he entered fearlessly, undeterred and determined not to slow down.

Further up ahead, the queen drone with Tarquini now hanging on for dear life suspended underneath it, had re-entered the nature reserve. The Flying Cootsman, with Peregrine and Olive sat on board, had already hurtled across the River Babble Bridge with such force that one of Tarquini's warning signs marked with a footprint, spun around uncontrollably as a result of it getting caught in the train's passing slipstream. The engine driver and sole passenger showed the most determined expressions knowing that they were closing in on their prey. Up ahead, they could see the queen drone struggling for power under the weight of its cumbersome passenger, reduced almost to a complete stop. The netting covering the reserve canopy now created an eerie atmosphere, somewhat similar to a fun fare ghost train ride. The Flying Cootsman could see its prey and slowed down to stalk it. Tarquini's alarmed shouts could be heard echoing from above. "Get me back to the manor house, Dotty! Dotty! Dotty!"

Inside the mansion, Dotty picked up Tarquini's desperate cry for help but couldn't see anything through the queen drone's remote camera except for obliterating clouds of steam. She leaned towards the monitor for a clearer view and began to tap the keyboard in desperation, only to send them the wrong way again further into the forest, back in the direction of the River Babble Bridge. "What on earth are you doing you stupid moronic woman?" Tarquini screamed at the top of his voice.

Deeply offended by Tarquini's remark and out of pure frustration, Dotty responded by picking up the keyboard and throwing it directly at the queen drone's monitor, and as a result both smashed into pieces on impact. "Well now you're on your own, you stupid moronic man. You can stay up there forever as far as I'm concerned!" She then ran across the hall landing into Tarquini's dressing room and in one single move, gathered up his entire collection of antique watches neatly displayed on top of a set of drawers. Peering back into Tarquini's nerve centre study she yelled, almost in retaliation, towards the broken screens, "Come on, Dotty, let's get out of here," before grabbing her pre-packed case and stuffing his watches into it. She fled from the study and scampered down the stairs and outside towards her sports car. Somewhat relieved by the fact that she had left the melee behind and was escaping from the scene, Dotty reached her sports car only to find that each tyre had been punctured.

Completely unaware of Dotty's sudden exit, Tarquini diplomatically changed his tone. "Dotty? Dotty? Dotty? Are you still there, my precious pumpkin? Your Tarky Warky didn't mean to Barky, Barky at you!" he pleaded, hanging perilously onto the drone by one hand and clutching the trophy with the other. The queen drone was limping erratically under the strain and now completely out of control underneath the enclosed canopy.

Still standing there aghast at her vandalised car, Dotty let out an almighty accusative cry. "I bet this was your work, you ghastly Adamsons!" Thinking on her feet she made a quick mobile call to Tarquini's associate, Harry the Fence, only to find Harry's phone engaged. However, she left a message explaining her predicament. "Hello Harry, this is Dotty D'eath. Tarquini has asked me to call you and pass this message on to you as he's a little tied up and hanging around for someone at the moment." She let out a short snigger at her snide remark, "Apparently, there's been a change of plan and instead of the original booty he wanted you to flog on the black market, he's now got a dozen or so rare antique wristwatches that have come into his hands and he wants you to find buyers for them. He said that only you know how to find such people apparently!" Dotty couldn't help sniggering to herself again at her inadvertent joke as she ended her call before adding, "It's imperative that you get here without delay from your room at the Didsvale Hotel and meet me outside Kingfisher Cottage right away. We will then leave for London where Tarquini will catch us up at your home address. I can't wait to make your acquaintance for the first time!" For what it was worth, she then decided to try and use her deflated sports car as the fastest means to get to the gatehouse lodge. Throwing her case onto the rear seats she jumped in, started the engine and began to travel as fast as she could down the driveway, despite the obvious resistance from the four flat tyres. "I'm so sorry for having to do this to you, Tarky Warky, but you've brought all of this onto yourself, you silly man!" she said to herself accompanied by a sad regretful sniffle.

Back on the pursuing pump trolley, which was now passing Didsvale Manor and looping back towards the nature reserve, Toby found renewed energy after arriving at the sloping track section, which Libby had predicted, and shouted to her, "Well, one thing's for sure!"

"What's that?" she replied."

"When I put those Squawkerlingo codes for the jackdaw instructions into SMEW for Tarquini, I also put in some extra codes and instructions!"

"What were those?" Libby replied, still focussing through the telescope.

"Well, let me put it this way. Woodpeckers can cause a lot of damage when they peck at sports car tyres. Hopefully, that will stop our dear friends at Didsvale Manor having any means of escape!"

On realising what Toby had done, Libby laughed out loud. "That's brilliant, Toby. Absolutely brilliant!"

"Well. He's been picking our brains in so much, I thought we'd peck at her tyres and see how she likes it!" he replied as he started to press back on the trolley handle again, then noticing that the downward slope was making things much easier.

# Chapter 21
## Peregrine's Revenge

The Flying Cootsman was now crawling along the track at walking pace with the dangling Tarquini Scumbali no more than a few metres ahead with the blinded queen drone, desperately edging along at a snail's pace. The steam from the Flying Cootsman's piston valves hissed louder and louder as if in sheer anger at the suspended enemy above. Unable to escape from the snare of his own canopy netting, Tarquini attempted to guide the queen drone with the aid of his swinging legs away from the prowling steam engine beneath. Gradually, he was able to move his unresponsive hovering queen drone a few more metres at the same height until they were out of the steam-shrouded nature reserve forestation and closer to the River Babble Bridge. Assuming that Dotty was still at the controls and about to glide him back to safety, he cried out to Peregrine and Olive watching pitifully below, "Well. It's arrivederci from me, losers! OK Dotty, please get me out of this mess and back to the manor house, pronto please!" He waited for Dotty to take action. He waited and waited and waited until he realised that his game was nearly up.

Olive looked across at Professor Peregrine and suggested, "One more for good luck, Peregrine?" Knowing exactly what she meant, he showed one extended thumb of confirmation to her.

"Yes, Olive. One for good luck! Take good aim," he replied.

Olive lifted out the last acorn from her top dungaree pocket. Placing it carefully into the elastic hairband which she was still holding in the other hand she took aim. With amazing accuracy, the acorn pierced through the steam before hitting the queen drone's fast fading red power sensor, completely knocking out any last remaining signal it was receiving from the abandoned control room. As a result, the now condemned drone started to spiral downwards out of control and into the fast-flowing River Babble with a final almighty splash. Just before it did so, its ineffective arm released the hapless Scumbali, dispatching him and his precious trophy to the ground where he landed in a crumpled heap on the embankment just before the bridge and a mere few meters away from the vengeful hissing steam engine and her passengers, who had also come to a stop in the middle of the bridge. Scumbali picked up the now badly dented trophy he'd let go of and subsequently landed on, before looking up in disbelief towards Professor Peregrine Greylag, who sat at the controls adorned with the same cap and gown which he was wearing at the time of the bicycle accident that Scumbali had forced him into. "Remember me, Scumbali?" Peregrine asked. He then deliberately edged the hissing Flying Cootsman towards Tarquini, forcing him to retreat steadily backwards until he was nearly at the end of the bridge, just to one side of the track. Peregrine continued. "Do you remember setting your drones on me just after I overheard you and Dotty D'eath making your dastardly illegal plans, and discovered the contents of your truck? Well, Scumball Scumbali. It looks as though your evil plans have come back to haunt you. In more ways than one!" Then, with one final command Peregrine let out a loud cry, "OK Argyll, do your deed!"

From his stooped, cowering position directly in front of the steam engine, the dumbfounded Tarquini Scumbali could only stare in disbelief, unable to muster a single word of reply. A loud caw could then be distinctly heard above the Flying Cootsman's unforgiving hissing. As Tarquini looked upwards, he noticed a large single black feather spiralling downwards until it ironically rested squarely on his forehead. The nearby reeds by the river began to stir slightly and unexpectedly in the still evening air. Within seconds, this slight breeze turned into a strong wind before a virtual hurricane swept in. Then, firstly up above appeared a flock of hundreds of jackdaws, who were followed by the approaching mighty Argyll, who had responded to Ahab's call. The jackdaws flew over, then together in small groups landed onto Tarquini's tree netting and by clawing away at it, lifted it up piece by piece from the tree canopy.

# Chapter 22
## Dotty Makes Haste

Back at Didsvale Manor, Dotty D'eath had managed to drive her erratically wobbling sports car down the manor drive towards the estate exit at Kingfisher Cottage, saying to herself on the way, "You're nearly there, Dotty, keep going!" No sooner had the words come from her mouth than she heard cawing noises coming from behind. Looking in her rear mirror, she noticed that they were the caws of pursuing jackdaws and started turning the steering wheel from side to side in an attempt to shake them off. "Go away, you horrid things," she screeched at them. Up ahead, she could see an immaculate luxury limousine, with what was apparently Harry the Fence at the wheel of their soon-to-be getaway car. It was parked just up ahead on the manor side of the cattle grid. "Thank God, for Harry the Fence! I've never been so pleased to see anyone in my whole life," she said to herself. With her punctured tyres now almost giving up the fight and reduced to splintering pieces of rubber, the treasured sports car came to an undignified halt immediately behind the parked limo. Dotty grabbed the suitcase off the back seat with one hand and opened the car door with the other. Each and every staggering step she took approaching Harry, was a step towards escape and freedom. Harry had conveniently turned his limo around for their quick departure and Dotty could only make out the back outline of the driver's head, displaying a generous amount of strangely familiar black wavy hair. Dotty finally made it to the safety of her awaiting accomplice to find the door fully opened for her arrival. She leapt into the front passenger seat with her suitcase without looking towards the driver, and pushed the suitcase with her shoulder to force it unceremoniously onto the back seat. Dotty then turned to the driver's seat and noticed that Harry the Fence was donning a white silk facemask and focussing directly ahead. She assumed this was his means to guard against identification whilst in the neighbourhood. Harry turned towards Dotty, whose eyebrows began to furrow from deeply engaging in thought at the familiar hair and sparkling brown eyes, which were now staring directly into her own wide-opened eyes. Harry then began to pull his mask away with a single hand forcing Dotty into a state of shock and surprise. After finally overcoming her bewilderment, she began to speak, "Tarky Warky! How on earth did you get here? I didn't mean to betray you. I only wanted what was best for both of us."

"Shut up, you stupid woman!" came the abrupt reply.

She continued to stare incredulously at the apparent miraculous appearance of Tarquini Scumbali in his posh limo. As they prepared to drive across the cattle grid by Kingfisher Cottage, their escape route was cut off by a bombardment of green netting. The same green netting that Scumbali had deviously covered the reserve tree canopy with, only now for the revengeful jackdaws to transfer it, clump by clump, onto the motionless vehicle below them, with Harry the Fence and Dotty D'eath completely incarcerated within and hollering frantically for their freedom.

The jackdaws cawed away uncontrollably at the result as if realising the poetic justice of their mission, having deposited the same green netting that had covered their own canopy nests and then to see it covering Dotty D'eath in revenge.

# Chapter 23
## *Tarquini's Demise*

Over by River Babble Bridge, and still completely struck with fear, with his head turned towards the developing shadow of Argyll's delta-shaped wings, Tarquini cowered from the hurricane-force downdraft of its delta-shaped wings. Peregrine and Olive watched as the mighty bird's massive wingspan swooped towards them overhead, getting closer and closer. Then suddenly, from behind them all, bursting through the steam of the Flying Cootsman, came Captain Ahab in full freewheel acceleration on Peregrine's bike with his heavy rucksack helping with his momentum. "Coming through! Mind the gap!" he shouted loudly at the amazed steam engine cab's occupants. Ahab rattled across the wooden river bridge footpath, swiftly approaching Tarquini who was now preoccupied with Argyll's appearance. In response to the trundling noise of the bridge's wooden planks rattling under Ahab's presence, Tarquini turned around to see a bike and a gigantic figure descend on him for a split second before the impact forced him to his release his grip on the weighty trophy and hurl him off the bridge and into the rushing River Babble below. The evading trophy, now spinning uncontrollably through the air, finally came back to earth with a crash and spilt out a small cloth bag from inside its damaged base. Peregrine's bike and its rider had come to an abrupt halt to watch the flailing Tarquini struggling in the racing waters.

"Help me. Please help me! I can't swim," Tarquini yelled. Before anyone could rustle up any mercy and attempt to rescue him, the rushing waters managed to sweep him alongside the Pretty Pol moored up nearby. Grasping a rung on a hanging rope ladder, he hauled himself up and onto the ship's deck before clinging onto the mast for firm footing against the raging downdraft caused by Argyll's wings. In the distance he could hear Olive's taunting voice come booming at him from the bridge. "Hey Scumbali. What's the word for a group of jackdaws?"

Within a split-second Peregrine jumped in with the answer with an equally loud response also in Scumbali's direction. "A train Scumbali, a TRAIN! The two laughed out uncontrollably at their perfect double-act sarcastic timing.

Tarquini Scumbali listened to the incoming sarcasm while sobbing and muttering helplessly to himself, "I loathe those pesky Adamsons." However, the tiny boat couldn't hold fast any longer from the hurricane force. With her sail billowed to bursting point, she broke her moorings to be swept downstream along the River Babble. Tarquini clung onto the mast for dear life, and with his legs trailing horizontally behind him, the Pretty Pol was blown to the river estuary before entering the open sea. She then quickly disappeared over the horizon, with Argyll's gigantic wings flapping effortlessly behind.

As Tarquini's demise was taking place, there came the grinding sound of metal on metal from the rear of the Flying Cootsman as Toby and Libby crashed into the back of the engine. Despite the gradient down towards the river, Toby had managed to slow the freewheeling pump trolley down sufficiently with his trailing foot but not enough to avoid a collision with the rear of the stationary engine, spilling both of them onto the adjoining footpath. In doing so, Libby once again caught the telescope on the edge of the pump trolley as she fell, causing the end to unscrew itself off completely. Cursing herself she said, "Blast! I'm so sorry, Peregrine. I'll have it repaired and as good as new for you, promise!" As she went to re-screw the end back onto its thread, she could see that a piece of paper had dislodged from inside the casing and was poking out by a few millimetres. She glanced at it inquisitively for a brief second and then rather than picking it out further with her fingers and having more important matters to attend to, she quickly pushed the paper back in again before re-screwing the end until it jammed back in as best as possible. She and Toby then got up and sprinted unerringly through the swirling steam, which was still hissing out of the engine, towards the cab at the front. Then, trying to peer through it, shouted together, "Is that you in there, Olive?"

"Yes, it's US," came Olive's familiar voice.

As the steam cloud cleared away, Libby could see the lone figure of her daughter sat in the engine cab and said quizzically, "What do you mean, US?"

Olive turned to notice that Professor Peregrine was no longer there and shouted at the empty seat now beside her, "Peregrine? Peregrine? Where are you?" she then turned, rambling to her parents. "It was Professor Peregrine! You must believe me! He helped us to get the Flying Cootsman here after I'd posted the happy memory postcard into the Silver Dream Machine part of the SMEW console and then Peregrine got the jackdaws to help us. How else do you think we got here?" she pleaded.

"Well of course we believe you Olive. I wouldn't put anything past this place any longer!" Toby said, glancing at Libby, before they jointly shrugged their shoulders signalling their joint belief in her explanation. Libby brought Peregrine's telescope up to her eye once again. As she did so, she read out the inscription on the key label still draped around her neck and muttered, " *'Keep your eye on the Prize!'* Well, I wouldn't say that Tarquini Scumbali is the best prize I've ever seen." It was only then that she recalled the piece of paper wound up inside the barrel of the telescope. Gripping, and then pulling with her fingernails, centimetre by centimetre, the mysterious piece of paper came more into view, until she held in one hand what appeared to be a rolled-up piece of ancient parchment. With Toby looking over her shoulder, she slowly began to flatten it out on the side of the Flying Cootsman's boiler. Libby studied the content and whispered it out to herself line by line. "So, that's why Peregrine wasn't wearing his telescope when Ahab found him! He knew somehow that his life might have been in danger when he visited Didsvale Manor and that must be why he decided to hide it in the engine shed before he left so Scumball Scumbali wouldn't find it!" She looked over at Toby and Olive eagerly awaiting to hear what had surprised her so much and exclaimed to them. "I hope you're both ready for this!"

As she finished the last words Toby responded. "Well this changes things completely! Unbelievable!"

Ahab swiftly returned, referring to Tarquini's departure saying, "Well it's good riddance to him." He then began to scan the parchment himself before raising one hand to his mouth in shock. As he did so, a small tear tumbled down one cheek. Not with sadness but from complete joy!

By this time, Olive had jumped down from the engine's cab. She retrieved the silver trophy and its small hidden bag from where they had fallen. She untied a small chord holding the cloth bag together and let out a huge cry as the contents spilt out in her hand. "Wow! Mum, Dad. Come over here quickly! Look at these!"

In next to no time, Constable Walker, who had been helping to bring normality to the manic scene back at the village hall, sprang onto the scene. "Have we missed anything?" queried the constable. Libby rolled up the piece of parchment and held it behind her back and away from the constable's prying eyes.

"Oh! Not much really," replied Toby understatedly.

The constable strode across to Olive and took one look at the glittering gemstones in her hand. "And where did you find these, young lady?" he asked.

"They came out of that!" she replied, pointing at the dilapidated trophy lying nearby. Constable Walker immediately recognised the trophy snatched from the grasp of the Honeysuckle sisters earlier when being presented to them by Tarquini Scumbali.

"Well, they look like they could be the diamonds stolen from the jewellers in the next village several weeks ago." He then mused to himself for a few seconds before drawing an adept deduction. "I think we need to speak to Tarquini Scumbali. Anyone here know of his whereabouts?"

In response to his question, Olive began to raise her arm and pointed hopelessly into the distance to where Tarquini was last seen departing in the direction of Pamona Atoll seen departing. "He went that way!"

Constable Walker looked confused by Olive's vague reply before responding with an encouraging wink towards her and saying, "On the plus side young lady. I'm sure there will be a very handsome reward waiting for the person responsible for finding these extremely valuable gemstones."

In the meantime, Nellie Buchanan, ambitiously wishing to add to her headline-hitting story, had sprinted directly towards Didsvale Manor from the Village Hall for an assumingly exclusive interview with Tarquini Scumbali. However, she only got as far as Kingfisher Cottage where she was confronted by a large netting-enshrouded car positioned on the cattle grid with Dotty D'eath's sports car immediately behind it. She could just about make out the familiar figures of the two desperate occupants attempting to claw their way out. In the distance, she could see the strange spectacle of the manor house also completely enshrouded in green netting left by the jackdaws! Nellie scribbled furiously away on her notepad, describing the whole scene and incriminating voice conversing from inside the car, saying, "Tarquini never told me he had an identical twin brother. Identical in appearance and identical in devious nature it seems. Anyway, we're both in this pickle and must escape from this god forbidden place forever!"

Hearing the commotion from the nearby River Babble bridge, and the prospect of the third scoop in a single day, Nellie suddenly stopped scribbling. Placing the notebook back into her pocket, she turned on her heels and made off towards where it was coming from.

Realising that someone was now in close proximity to the car, Dotty's sole voice could be heard whimpering desperately from inside, "Hello? Is there someone there? Please help us!"

Nellie shouted back in response as she left the scene, "It's

OK, Dotty. I'm going to get help from Constable Walker!"

Nellie was now well out of hearing distance when Dotty's blubbering words shouted out with further desperation. "No! We don't want that kind of help, you stupid girl."

Nellie dashed across the reserve to join the others to hopefully add to her exclusive story. Constable Walker made haste to Kingfisher Cottage after hearing Nellie's account of the unfolding scene there. Nellie was then left to scribble each and every one of Olive's excitable words as she recounted again and again the entire dramatic events that had happened around Didsvale.

# Chapter 24
## Six Years Later

The Flying Cootsman's distinctive tooting horn reverberated all around the park as she came to a gradual steam-filled halt into the Mighty Oak Tree Station with Lord Didsvale sitting in the engine driver's cab. The eccentric school cap and gown regularly worn by Professor Peregrine Greylag, were well-recognised features within Didsvale Park and Nature Reserve as he drove his miniature steam trains around the park and manor estate. Today though was a very special occasion. After the earlier '*Younoseeme Squibrel Show*' which enthralled the younger children. Lots of grown-ups and children stepped down from the packed tiny rear passenger carriages and hurried towards the open-air auditorium to take their seats. "Hurry up Tarquin and Harry! We don't want to miss Olive," said one anxious parent to his children. He turned around to reveal a swarthy Mediterranean appearance. His slim, long dark-haired and overly dressed wife tottered clumsily behind him on high-heeled shoes down from the station platform. They could quite easily have been two eccentric comedy characters from a novel!

The mighty oak tree was a fitting backdrop for Didsvale Park's special '*Young Writer's Master Class Presentation*', and Professor Peregrine's old bike had been propped up against the tree for theatrical effect. Tickets were sold out well in advance for the early evening event being held in the park's sun-bathed glade. Not a single empty seat was to be seen amongst the packed audience as the start drew near. Every Didsvale villager seemed to be there.

Nodding directly to many familiar faces in the audience directly in front of her, Olive Adamson sat confidently awaiting her prompt as guest speaker. She brought out from her pocket her lucky omen compass and placed it directly onto the table in front of her. Two faces in particular smiled back belonging to her proud parents, who sat together on the front row donning their Didsvale Ranger uniforms. Also sat there beaming, was her best friend, Nellie Buchanan. Stood to one side, a dapper-dressed giant of a man began to speak. "As Didsvale Park and Nature Reserve Director I'm honoured to present to you this evening's guest speaker and recent recipient of *'Didsvale Village Young Story Writer of the Year Award'*. Please put your hands together for Olive Adamson!" Olive rose confidently from her seat, consumed by the loud applause from the enthusiastic audience. The thing that made it extra special this year to the audience was that the recipient was one of their own local villagers.

"Thank you, Mr Ahab McCrab! It's a privilege to be invited here and the opportunity to tell you all about my story, and how I came to write it. I'll be more than happy to ask questions at the end. Thank you," she said. More applause rang out in response before dying down to a respectful silence as she began to speak, "It feels like just five minutes ago when my family and I were so warmly welcomed into Didsvale Village. I remember the invitation you sent to my parents as we were moving into Kingfisher Cottage asking if they'd like to consider being volunteer park wardens, and if I wanted to come and see the enchanting Younoseeme Squibrel Show with all the other enchanted children. It's great to see that the show is still going strong and Professor Peregrine Greylag is still working his magic. This evening would not have been possible without the professor and his incredible Flying Cootsman steam engine, over there, who are still going strong today I'm pleased to see!" She gave a gentle wave of her hand towards Peregrine, standing keenly on the footplate of the Flying Cootsman. He doffed his cap in acknowledgment to the applauding gathering as he placed one finger on his lip and patted the boiler of his steam engine, as if asking for them to keep the true secrets of his magic show and the Flying Cootsman just to themselves. For the next hour or so, Olive kept the audience transfixed with her speech, who hung onto her every single word, before concluding her presentation. "So, I thought I would make Harry the Fence into Tarquini Scumbali's twin brother at the end, just to add a little bit of extra twist and suspense. But it was right that justice prevailed for both him and the eccentric Dotty D'eath in the end after being found guilty and sent to prison for a very long time. Where is the evil Tarquini Scumbali? Well, I reckon that if you look closely enough out to the horizon, you may catch sight of him desperately waving from the top of one of those wind farm turbines on the distant horizon," she giggled. "And we all know that the ever-dependable Pretty Pol is safely back here taking visitors up and down the River Babble on her nature cruises as many of you have enjoyed today. You all know what was written on the mysterious piece of parchment that Libby found hidden within the telescope? Well, it was the ancient deed declaring that under no circumstances could Didsvale Manor estate and Didsvale Park ever be sold, but instead bequeathed to the villagers of Didsvale and other local charities in perpetuity, as we all acknowledge to this day. "Yes, dear villagers of Didsvale, it only seems a fleeting moment that I fell asleep and into that strange limbo-slumber world hovering between reality and fantasy in my bedroom at Kingfisher Cottage that day and encountered the phenomenon that is the deep blue vortex! But wait a minute!" she stopped herself abruptly, enticing the audience with baited breath into what she was going to say. "Yes, but wait a minute! I clearly remember one other thing as though it was only yesterday! Just before I fell asleep, I really did see that starling murmuration in the sky writing those words to me! Because how did I know so much about Didsvale Park before the actual event, which led to me writing this story? Was it a premonition, déjà vu, second sight, or a combination of them all? Wouldn't it be nice if we could all have a 'Silver Dream Machine' like Professor Peregrine's, and the means to bring back happy memories from the past back into the present with an old cherished photograph? Why don't you all try placing a happy memory photograph of your own under your pillow tonight before you go to sleep. Who knows where it may take you! And that includes mums and dads!" she added with a broad smile at her parents. "I shall leave that for all your imaginations. Thank you all for coming this evening to listen to my presentation and maybe—for knowing what I was going to say!" she added humorously.

The audience nodded in appreciation at the end of her enthralling presentation before breaking out into spontaneous applause. As Olive heard the applause echoing deep within her concentrated mind and then dying down, she looked at the label on the key hanging around her neck displaying the words

*'Writing Desk'*, on one side and *'Seek and you shall find'* on the other. With one hand she felt the outline of a 'Y'-shaped branch and a single acorn still nestling in her dungaree pocket.

Just about poking out of another pocket was a postcard she'd purchased from the souvenir shop on the way in and entitled—*OPENING CEREMONY—FLYING COOTSMAN IN SUNSET ON THE RIVER BABBLE BRIDGE.*

She then retrieved her lucky compass and placed it back into her pocket without noticing that the needle inside had begun to swivel erratically!

From the driver's cab of the Flying Cootsman, Peregrine tapped away at his laptop keypad, which he had earlier programmed. The roof of a lorry parked nearby opened very slowly from his commands and its contents began to emerge upwards. Then, high above the tree canopy and against the backdrop of the darkening evening, dozens of drones whirred around providing an amazing choreographed drone light show, which surprised and entertained the whole audience for the remainder of the evening. The illuminated drones arranged themselves into groups of synchronised and choreographed aerial formations, making clever shapes of Professor Peregrine Greylag on the footplate of the Flying Cootsman in full steam with her carriages behind, before each of the station names around the park also came into view. These then changed into the outlines of various birds from the nature reserve. Next, the distinct outline of Captain Ahab McCrab could be seen, to the delight of the onlookers, and the shape of Bosun's Cabin. The drones then joined up as one to create the shape of a gigantic tree and as a final encore, broke away in all directions only to reform into a series of letters and words. The audience broke out into spontaneous applause as one by one they made out the bright laser wording in the sky accompanied by the shapes of three small keys...

## CONGRATULATIONS TO OLIVE ADAMSON FROM PROFESSOR PEREGRINE GREYLAG AND ALL OF DIDSVALE

As the applause died down and people started to make their way home, Professor Peregrine Greylag looked down at a recent copy of The Didsvale Dynamo newspaper occupying the empty seat next to him. With its front-page headline and story just about legible, he chuckled to himself...

## DIDSVALE PARK DECLARED PROTECTED SITE OF NATIONAL HERITAGE!

*An ancient parchment found inside a hollow in one of the park's ancient oak tree's upper boughs has been declared of national historical importance. The parchment contained a map confirming the precise location of a fabled prehistoric tree directly underneath the park's miniature railway engine shed. Tree roots extending down into a seemingly bottomless labyrinth were discovered there and emanating a mysterious green and brown glow. The parchment was found by one of the park's inspection drones during a recent safety audit of the park. Didsvale Park's Manager, Ahab McCrab quotes. "We regularly use these drones to inspect both the park and the nearby nature reserve to ensure that our miniature railway and wildlife attractions are safe for all of our visitors. We have built a glass viewing-platform underneath the engine shed's turntable for visitors far and wide to witness this wonderful phenomenon. All extra proceeds from this attraction will be invested in the miniature railway, bird hides for the nature reserve and for the upkeep of our beloved Pretty Pol and her cruises along the River Babble. It's wonderful that this discovery will safeguard Didsvale Park's future forever."*

*At the time of press, Lord Didsvale (Professor Peregrine Greylag) was unavailable for comment very busy working on a long-term miniature steam engine renovation project.*

## The End

(Well, that is unless your limbo slumber happy memory deep blue vortex knows differently of course!)